ENMITY

An enthralling Scottish murder mystery

PETE BRASSETT

THE BOOK FOLKS

Paperback published by The Book Folks

London, 2017

© Pete Brassett

This book is a work of fiction. Names, characters, businesses, organizations, places and events are either the product of the author's imagination or are used fictitiously. Any resemblance to actual persons, living or dead, events or locales is entirely coincidental. The spelling is British English.

ISBN 978-1-5207-2342-6

www.thebookfolks.com

ENMITY is the third novel by Pete Brassett to feature detectives Munro and West. Look out for SHE, the first book, and AVARICE, the second. It is followed by DUPLICITY, TERMINUS, TALION and PERDITION. All of these titles can be enjoyed on their own, or as a series.

Chapter 1

For those whose culinary prowess was limited to opening a tin of beans or grilling the occasional slice of cheese on toast, the tiny kitchen, with no natural light and a broken oven, was ideal. Crammed side by side along the back wall sat the sink – filled with empty beer cans; the cooker – its white, enamelled surface coated in a thin layer of sticky, brown grease; and the fridge – wedged tightly between two ageing, dilapidated cupboards.

He stood in his underwear clutching a heavy, copper-based saucepan in his right hand and stared at the last of his provisions sitting on the worktop: half a pint of milk, a knob of butter and two brown, speckled eggs. The only decision he had to make was: fried, boiled, poached or scrambled? He spun the pan by the handle as he contemplated his options. Frying involved oil, of which he had none. Boiling or poaching used only water and therefore meant little or no washing-up. Scrambled, however, for some bizarre reason, seemed to make the eggs go further and would also ensure neither the milk nor the butter would go to waste. He chose scrambled and brought the pan down hard, smashing the eggs to smithereens and splattering himself and the worktop with dollops of bright, yellow yolk and sticky, white albumen in the process. Sneering, he dropped the pan to the floor, showered and dressed for work.

* * *

Andrew Maxwell Stewart, "Max" to those who knew him, cursed as he forced himself into his suit which, he'd been assured, was cut in a style deemed to be *de rigueur* for someone in his profession, despite his reflection telling him it belonged on somebody six inches shorter. The ridiculously slim-fitting jacket inhibited any kind of movement from the elbow up and the trousers, he was sure, would in time be responsible for a low sperm count. He counted his blessings that he didn't have to bend to lace up his shoes and slipped on a pair of loafers.

The short walk to Beresford Terrace and the estate agency where he idled away the working day, was fraught with the usual obstacles, in particular the hordes of zombies who bumbled along with their heads buried in their phones, fearful of missing another "tweet", a "like", or, God forbid, a photo of what their "friends" ate for dinner the night before. He paused by the door, took a deep breath, and walked inside.

* * *

The receptionist, a young, lissom brunette by the name of Lizzie, thought of him as sartorially elegant and, with his ruffled hair and two days' worth of stubble on his boyish, pointed chin, the epitome of "ruggedly handsome". She would have been wise, however, to heed the adage involving books and covers for beneath his polished exterior lay the only pair of socks and the only pair of shorts he possessed, neither of which had been washed in days.

'Alright Max?' she said, smiling coyly, batting her eyelids.

'Aye, not bad,' said Max, 'you?'

'I'm okay. Listen, I was thinking, it's nearly a month since you joined the firm and we've still not been out for that "welcome-aboard" drink, have we?'

'No, no, you're quite right. We haven't.'

'So, how about it? After all, it is Friday. We'll not have to be up in the morning.'

'Sorry hen, but I've plans already,' said Max, lying.

'Oh,' said Lizzie, disappointed, 'is it…? I imagine you must have a date?'

'No, no. Nothing like that.'

'Oh good, I mean, it must be your girlfriend, then.'

'Dinnae have one,' said Max, 'I've, er, I've a pal down, that's all. Been meaning to catch up for ages, cannae get out of it.'

'Och, well, I know what that's like. Maybe… maybe if you're not doing anything tomorrow…'

'Tomorrow? Saturday? Aye, okay. Maybe. I'll let you know.'

* * *

Max sighed as he pulled off his jacket, flicked on the computer and waited for the ping which would invariably herald the arrival of precisely zero emails. He checked his watch against the clock on the wall. It was 9:15am.

'Coffee?' he said, making his way to the kitchenette.

'Aye, thanks very much,' said Lizzie. 'So, what's on your schedule today?'

'Same as yesterday.'

'Oh, dear, is it that quiet?'

'Aye, but it's not up to me to drum up business, is it? That's down to your boss.'

'Right enough, I suppose. Do you not get a wee bit bored?'

'Bored? Are you joking me? All the time. Every day. This job is killing me.'

'Och, it's not that bad, is it? Getting paid to sit around doing nothing, it's easy.'

'It's crap. It's for folk with no drive, no ambition and no self-esteem. No offence, like.'

'Doesnae bother me,' said Lizzie, as Max struggled with his jacket, 'but I'm just paid to answer the… are you off out?'

'Aye, I'm away for my lunch.'

'Lunch? But you've only just come in.'

'Alright then, breakfast. Can I get you something?'

'No, you're alright, I've got mine here.'

'What? More dried fruit and peanuts I suppose?'

'Aye, what's wrong with that?'

'I've seen a pigeon with a gastric band eat more than you.'

'I'm watching my weight. Besides, it's healthy.'

'Of course it is. So is looking like a stick insect.'

'Have I done something to offend you?'

Max paused by the door and frowned as he rubbed his forehead.

'No,' he said, 'look, I'm sorry, I didnae mean to… I'm just… I get irritable when I've not eaten. See you later.'

* * *

Much to his relief, the walk from the office up to Alloway Street was mercifully quiet, caught as it was in the lull between the shops opening for business and the inevitable lunchtime rush comprising workers craving their tuna mayos and steak pies, and pensioners on a mission to browse the department stores without spending a penny. He ambled, hands in pockets against the brisk breeze blowing in from the coast, until he reached the ATM. Reluctantly, he offered up his card and requested a balance. Overdrawn. Pay day – a weekend away. Against his better judgement, he withdrew £80, tucked £20 into his wallet for safe keeping and headed for the bookies three doors down.

A row of gambling machines, each with the enticing lure of a £500 pay-out, sat idle, waiting for someone gullible enough to sate their voracious appetites. Max, more of an optimist than an addict, duly obliged and emerged nine minutes later, £60 poorer and a great deal angrier. He pulled out his antiquated phone and called the office.

'Lizzie, listen hen, my phone's about to die on me so I cannae talk long, I've got a lead on a place coming on the market. I think I can poach it off the other agents so if I'm not back, don't worry. I'll see you Monday, okay?'

'Okay,' said Lizzie, 'but what about… I mean, do you think you fancy that drink?'

'Aye, text me your number and I'll give you a call.'

* * *

Waterstone's on the high street was, to Max, one of life's havens and the only place he could go, apart from the library or his flat, where he could sit undisturbed in detached solitude. He headed straight to "Philosophy", plucked a copy of Plato's *Symposium* from the shelf and settled down in an all-too-comfortable armchair. Any desire for lunch soon passed as he sat engrossed in the varying definitions of love proffered by the collection of poets, writers, physicians and statesmen, oblivious to the steady trickle of literary enthusiasts who huffed indignantly as they navigated their way around him.

A middle-aged lady, smartly dressed in a grey blouse and black pencil skirt, slipped silently into the chair beside him, crossed her legs and watched, fascinated, as his face contorted with concentration. Max, aware of her presence, turned and slowly raised his eyes, settling on the badge pinned to her chest proclaiming "Manageress".

'Hola guapo,' she said softly.

''Scuse me?'

'Not being funny, but this isn't a library.'

Max, miffed by the interruption, stared into her dark, brown eyes.

'Aye, and we're not in Barcelona, either,' he said. 'What's your point?'

'Are you going to buy that book or not?'

5

'I'm not sure. I havenae finished it yet.'

'That's not how it works.'

'Look,' said Max, 'if it's what I'm looking for, I'll buy it. Okay?'

'And what are you looking for?' said the manageress, intrigued.

'Answers.'

'Answers? To what, exactly?'

'Life. Love.'

'And you think they're in there?'

'Aye, maybe,' said Max, enthusiastically flicking back to the fourth speech, 'see here, Aristophanes, you know what he says about love?'

'Enlighten me,' said the manageress, warming to him.

'He says that humans were originally created with four arms and four legs and a head with two faces, and that they were incredibly powerful and clever, so much so that they were capable of reaching the heavens and unseating the gods.'

'Is that so?'

'Aye, so the council of gods, they were that scared, see, that Zeus came up with a plan to enfeeble them. He split them in two, into two separate beings, each with two arms, two legs and one face and in doing so, he condemned them to spend their entire lives searching for their other halves.'

'I see.'

'So love is the name for our pursuit of wholeness, for our desire to be whole.'

'That's quite profound,' said the manageress, slowly uncrossing her legs, 'but my desire is to turn a profit.'

'What good is a profit if you've no-one to share it with?'

The manageress stood and shimmied as she pulled down her skirt.

'Keep the book,' she said, 'it's on me.'

Max sat back and regarded her inquisitively, charmed by her coquettish smile.

'Tell me, Miss Manageress,' he said frowning, 'are you whole, or are you searching?'

'Oh, I'm searching,' she said with a wink, 'still searching.'

* * *

Max, having devoured the book in its entirety, sighed as he contemplated the wisdom of Plato, certain only that the answers he sought were too many to comprehend in one sitting. His checked his phone: 17:06. One message – Lizzie Paton. A phone number, a smiley face and an "x". His lip curled at the thought. Not that he didn't like her, not that she wasn't attractive, he simply wasn't interested. He glanced at the manageress as he left, returning her blush with an empathetic smile.

The walk back to his flat above the shop on Main Street, punctuated by a pause on the bridge across the Ayr, another at the chippy to pick up a fish supper and a third for six cans of Stella, was pleasant enough. The odour coming from the kitchen as he opened the door was not. It reminded him of school, the kind of smell unleashed by the stink-bombs he used to lob around the playground before being expelled for unruly behaviour and a complete inability to concentrate in class.

Realising there were limits to the degree of squalor he was willing to tolerate, he set his bags on the table, grabbed a tee-shirt from the pile of dirty laundry sitting on the bathroom floor and grudgingly set about mopping up the mess. Satisfied his efforts were borderline acceptable, he tossed the shirt in the bin and, in the absence of a television, sat down to eat his supper with classical music drifting from the radio and a copy of Machiavelli's *The Prince* propped up before him.

As was his routine after dinner, he added the empty beer cans to the collection in the sink, binned the remnants of his haddock and chips and headed out for a walk towards the river. By night, crossing the bridge was, he thought, like travelling through a portal to another world. Forsaking the relative peace of Main Street, he immersed himself in the hustle and bustle of Sandgate, teaming with after-work revellers intent on drinking themselves into oblivion. He stopped on the corner of St. John Street, arrested by the sight of a girl wearing the briefest of skirts, weaving from side to side as she teetered on a pair of vertigo-inducing heels, doing her best to remain upright. He shook his head in despair, bewildered that someone so young and so pretty could allow herself to get in to such a state. He stood, back against the wall as she approached, intent on giving her a wide berth but, as he expected, she careered into him like iron filings drawn to a magnet.

'Whoops!' she said, giggling, as he grabbed her by the shoulders. 'Sorry!'

'Nae bother,' said Max, overwhelmed by the scent of her perfume, 'are you okay?'

'Aye,' she said, throwing her arms around his neck, 'do you mind if I stop here a moment, get my balance?'

Max dropped his head, her hair smelled of Spring, he could feel the heat of her chest as it beat against his.

'I think you've had one too many,' he said, 'will I get you a taxi?'

'No, you're alright. I've not far to go.'

'Are you sure? Where are you staying?'

'Cathcart Street.'

'Just around the corner, then. Will I walk you back?'

'What are you? A knight in shining armour?'

'Maybe.'

'What's your name?'

'Max.'

'Well, Max, I'm Ness and I'm thankful. Can I lean on you? Is that okay?'

To all and sundry, they looked like any other regular couple returning home after a raucous night out, their gait steady and slow, she clinging to him for fear of falling, he wearing a smug expression, thinking himself fortunate to have such a girl on his arm. They stopped three doors from the end of the street.

'Hope you've not too many stairs to climb,' said Max, as she fumbled in her bag for a set of keys.

'Opposite direction,' said Ness grinning, 'basement flat. It's all downhill from here!'

'Okay, well, I'll be…'

'Hold on there, Max, will you not come in and take a drink?'

'No, no, you're alright,' said Max, 'I should go, it's getting late.'

'Late? Are you joking me? Come on, just a wee night cap, it won't kill you.'

Chapter 2

House breaking, vehicle theft and common assault constituted the bulk of D.S. Cameron's daily workload, all of which were invariably linked in one way or another to the burgeoning drugs market which, contrary to official figures, was rife in the area. Bodies, however, were something of a rarity.

In a single twelve-month period, he'd had to deal with just three. The first was an eighty-two-year-old pensioner found festering in her fly-ridden flat on the eleventh floor of a tower block who, having expired in her sleep, had lain undiscovered for several weeks, her absence of no concern to her neighbours. The second was a bloated carcass washed ashore with no visible signs of injury apart from those inflicted by the fish who'd delighted in feasting on his flesh as he bobbed on the ebb and flow of the tide before beaching like a whale on a rocky outcrop south of Troon. The third was a single, successful city worker found naked, dangling by a length of rope attached to a robe hook on the back of the bathroom door with a black bin liner taped tightly around his head. Autoerotic asphyxiation was a term, and a practice, that mystified him.

He ducked under the cordon strung across the open gate and shuffled down the concrete steps to the gloom of the basement flat below, overwhelmed by the niggling sensation that the fourth would not warrant the words "natural", "accidental" or "misadventure" on the death certificate.

The front door showed no sign of a forced entry leaving him to conclude that unless there was another way in, the victim either knew her assailant or the perpetrator had a set of keys. He moved to the lounge and glanced inside. Apart from a small green shoulder bag lying on the arm of the sofa and two empty tumblers sitting on the coffee table, there was nothing untoward. The stereo, volume down, was still on.

The flash of a camera drew him down the hall to the bedroom where a team of SOCOs were diligently dusting for prints and collating evidence. He leant against the doorway and shivered as his eyes settled on the body spread-eagled across the bed, the wrists and ankles bound to the bedposts, the sheet pulled down over the face. Her skirt, short as it was, was hitched up around the waist. Her legs, bare and bronzed from the application of a tanning agent were smooth and free from cuts or abrasions. He winced at the thought of what had probably occurred just a few hours earlier until realising, with a jolt, that her underwear was still intact, as was her top. Nothing had been removed, nothing was ripped or torn. She was, to all intents and purposes, fully clothed.

'What do you think?' he said, frowning at someone in a Tyvek suit scanning the victim's upper thighs with a forensic light source.

The figure switched off the FLS, stood upright and pulled down her face mask.

'And you are?'

'Cameron. D.S. Cameron. Don.'

'Well, Don,' she said, the strain showing in her eyes, 'she struggled, understandably, but at the moment, I can see no sign of any… interference.'

'You mean she wasnae…'

'No, at least I don't think so. The post-mortem will pick up anything I've missed but at this stage, I have to say, there doesn't appear to be anything sexual about this at all.'

'That's what bothers me,' said Cameron, perplexed, 'that's what makes it seem all the more…'

His words tailed off as he squatted by the bed to inspect the wounds around the ankles where the cords from a hair dryer and a phone charger had lacerated the skin leaving a gash on each leg approximately half an inch deep.

'Jesus,' he said, exasperated. 'She must've really… you know, for a wee cable, I mean, a plastic cable, to do that.'

'Aye,' said the SOCO, 'she certainly did her best. It's the same on the wrists. Whoever tied her up bound her up so tight he all but cut-off the blood supply. See here, the hands, they're turning black from the clots.'

Cameron stepped forward to get a closer look, grimacing at the sight of the fingers which, with the onset of rigor, were as dark and contorted as a raven's claws.

'How long?' he asked quietly.

'Eight. Ten hours, maybe. No more.'

'So, roughly between midnight and two o'clock this morning then?'

'Aye. About that,' said the SOCO, reaching for a pair of stainless steel shears. 'Will I cut her free?'

'Okay, may as well, I suppose. No! Hold on,' said Cameron, raising a hand. 'Hold on just a moment.'

'What is it?' said the SOCO.

'Her wrists. He's tied her up with cable ties.'

'Aye. So?'

'So, who walks around with just two cable ties in his pocket?'

'I've no idea. An electrician, maybe? Besides, perhaps he had more.'

'Then why use the flex from a hair dryer and a phone charger to tie her feet? Something's not right here. It's not as impulsive as it looks. Can you dust them? The cable ties?'

'Aye, of course, but I wouldnae hold your breath.'

'Why not?'

'I doubt they'd hold a print for a start. Also, whoever did this wore gloves. There's a barely print here that doesnae belong to her.'

'I see,' said Cameron, as he contemplated the cuts around the wrists. 'How about the lounge? The glasses on the coffee table?'

'We've not been there yet.'

'Fair enough. Fair enough.'

Cameron turned his head towards the sheet and bit his lower lip, his nose twitching as he eyed the dark brown stain above the victim's face.

'What's that?' he said. 'That stain, and that smell? Christ, it stinks like…'

'Judging by the colour,' said the SOCO, 'and as you say, the smell, I'd say it's probably vomitus.'

'Sorry?'

'Puke.'

'Right.'

'With a drop or two of blood.'

'You think she threw up?'

'Possibly,' said the SOCO with an exhausted sigh, 'and lying on her back like that, there's a good chance she choked on it if she did.'

'Nice.'

'Shall we take a look?'

Cameron rose to his feet and took a step back, not entirely sure what to expect.

'Aye okay, go ahead,' he said, as the SOCO raised the sheet, 'just warn me if it's anything... dear God! What the...?'

Chapter 3

D.S. West was not green-fingered. A little light-fingered as an errant youth, perhaps, trying to impress her peers in leafy suburbia, but when it came to foliage, plants to her were nothing more than things that grew in the countryside or sat in buckets outside petrol stations and, despite being what her parents called "the outdoors type", she'd never harboured an interest in cultivating them. Surprised, she stood back and admired her handiwork.

'Not a bad job, Charlie,' said Munro, regarding the flower bed, 'and I thought you didn't know your aster from your elderflower.'

'I don't,' she said with a satisfied grin, 'but I've just realised what I've been missing.'

'And what's that?'

'It's not just about sticking a flower in the ground, is it? It's all of this: the fresh air, the sun on your face, the creepy crawlies, being alone with your thoughts. There's something quite… therapeutic, about it.'

'At last you've got it, lassie. I take it this means you'll not be deriding the old folk when you see them tending their roses then?'

'No, I will not. Tell you what, though, it don't half give you an appetite, I'm absolutely…'

She paused, pulled her phone from her pocket, glanced at the screen and sighed as she shoved it back in her jeans.

'Not bad news, I hope,' said Munro.

'No. Well, yes. Kind of. It's that arse, Wilson.'

'D.C.I. Wilson?'

'One and the same. I'm supposed to be back on duty in two days and he can't help but remind me. Do you know that's the fourth message he's left today?'

'So, you're still not keen on going home then?'

'No, I am not, but I have to,' said West with a sigh, 'if only to hand in my notice. I simply cannot bear the thought of London anymore, the drunks and the druggies, the shouting and the leering. And that's just the lads in the station.'

'Well, why not request a transfer?'

'I need a vacancy first, James.'

'And by the look on your face, you've checked and…'

'Nothing, except Glasgow, and there's no point in carrying coals to Newcastle is there?'

'No, no, I suppose not.'

'Still, it's no big deal, I'll go down, give them my letter of resignation, then come back up again. Sorry, I'm being presumptuous. It is okay if I stay a while longer, isn't it? I mean, I wouldn't want to…'

Munro headed inside, smiling to himself.

'You can stay as long as you like, Charlie,' he said, 'I've told you before, you're most welcome here.'

'Thanks,' said West, following him, 'just till I get sorted, I'll be out of your way just as soon as…'

'Charlie,' said Munro, waving a bread knife, 'stop blethering, I'll not tell you again, you can stay as long as you like. Now, ham or cheese? Or can I tempt you with a compendium of sorts?'

* * *

Munro plonked a plate of thick-cut roast ham and Kintyre cheddar sandwiches on the table with a couple of mugs of tea and sat down, exhausted from heaving bags of compost around the garden. West sipped the steaming brew and stared thoughtfully into space.

'You know what?' she said, softly, 'I never told you this before but when I came up a couple of weeks ago, you know, to go to the Holy Isle? I actually had a mild panic attack on the ferry over.'

Munro looked surprised.

'A panic attack? You?' he said. 'Now, why would that be?'

'It's silly really. Pathetic even. I was worried that I wouldn't be able to cope without my email, or my phone, or the television. I was cacking myself. How stupid is that?'

'It's not stupid, Charlie. Folk are, generally speaking, averse to change, that's all it is. But change can be for the better. Point in fact, look behind you, what do you see?'

West swivelled in her chair.

'The window. And the sky. And the sea.'

'Aye. And that's all the television you'll ever need.'

West pushed her plate to one side and tapped her phone.

'I thought you'd learned to live without that,' said Munro, sarcastically.

'Very funny. Just checking he's not still harassing me. Plus, I want a quick look at the news, make sure we're not under nuclear attack or anything like that.'

'Och, you'll not need to look at your phone if that occurs, lassie. When the wind blows, you'll know about it. Personally, I never look myself, there's nothing joyous about the news, it's always bleak.'

'Well, you're not wrong there,' said West, 'more threats of strikes, more people whinging about salaries, more people you've never heard of filing for divorce and, oh, they've found a body. Up the road by the looks of it.'

'Is that so?'

'Yup, Ayr. That's up the road, isn't it? Young girl found dead in her flat.'

'Probably overdosed on some illegal drug peddled by a no good…'

'No, looks a bit more serious than that. They're appealing for witnesses at the moment. Her name's Craig. Student.'

'Craig?' said Munro, smiling wistfully, 'I used to work with a fellow called Craig, did I tell you that?'

'Where? In Dumfries?'

'Aye, at The Mount. Alexander Craig. He was a D.I. like myself, somewhat younger but a lovely chap, astoundingly clever. Jean and I would visit his home every month – for lunch on a Sunday. His wife, Elspeth, was quite the joker, lovely sense of humour.'

'Do you keep in touch?'

'Not without the aid of a clairvoyant,' said Munro, mournfully, 'he passed away not long ago.'

'Sorry,' said West, 'was it…?'

'No, no, nothing work related, if that's what you mean. It was the cancer that took him. Diagnosed on a Monday, dead on the Thursday.'

'Bloody hell, that's tragic. What about his wife?'

'A few months later,' said Munro, shaking his head, 'couldnae live without him, I suppose. Just his daughter left now, lovely girl, Agnes, she's called. Full of energy, could never make her mind up about anything; one minute it was university, the next, travel the world. A real flibbertigibbet. Aye, that's the word, flibbertigibbet. I wonder how she's getting on? What is it?'

West, not sure how to react, laid down her phone and tentatively pushed it across the table, watching as Munro's eyes narrowed in a bid to focus on the screen. He swallowed hard and walked to the window where he stood for a moment, hands clasped behind his back, and stared out to sea.

'I have to make a call,' he said as he marched determinedly to his study, 'there's a twelve-year-old in the sideboard. Fetch it, would you?'

Munro returned thirty minutes later, sat opposite West and lifted his glass.

'Cheers, Charlie. Your very good health,' he said, knocking back the malt.

'Are you okay?'

'Couldn't be better. Now, a word. Tonight, we're going to treat ourselves to a steak supper then you need to get your head down. We've an early start.'

'What do you mean?'

'We're away to Ayr, first thing. It's not far, won't take long.'

'But I can't,' said West, 'I told you, I have to get back to London and...'

'No longer necessary, lassie. As of now, you're on secondment and you're working with me. It's all been taken care of.'

Chapter 4

Unlike the more notable buildings in the city, most of which were hewn from sandstone and constructed with outstanding attention to detail, the police office on King Street exuded all the charm of an abandoned multi-storey car park built from Lego. Munro leaned forward and cringed as he peered up at the drab, concrete monstrosity from behind the windscreen.

'Dear God,' he muttered, 'if Mr. Mackintosh could see this, he'd be turning in his grave.'

'Who?' said West.

'Charles Rennie... och, never mind.'

* * *

The lobby, furnished with a single, artificial bamboo tree and an array of tired posters advising visitors of the perils of unlicensed taxis, bogus callers and driving whilst under the influence was, apart from a dishevelled figure straddling the only three chairs available, deserted. Munro regarded the ruffian and, with his unshaven face, vintage leather car coat and scuffed, brown boots, intuitively assumed him to be minus a probation officer. West, on the other hand, was drawn to the alluring inch-long scar running from the corner of his left eye, clearly the legacy of an altercation with a blade.

'I know you,' said the scruff as he tumbled from the chairs and hauled himself wearily to his feet.

'You must be confusing me with somebody else,' said Munro. 'Marlon Brando, perhaps?'

'No, no, if anything I'd say…'

'Careful.'

The man smiled and held out his hand.

'Don Cameron, chief. D.S. Don Cameron. And you must be Detective Sergeant…'

'Charlie,' said West with a smile. 'Charlie will do just fine.'

'Well, it's good to see you. The boss says you knew the young girl, is that right, sir?'

'Aye, I did. Her father and I worked together. I knew his family.'

'Well, it's no wonder you want to get involved and, I'm not ashamed to say, we could use the help.'

'Too much on your plate?' said West.

'Put it this way,' said Cameron, 'I hope you're not keen on sleeping at regular intervals.'

West raised her eyebrows.

'Depends on the company.'

'Good grief,' said Munro. 'You'll have to excuse her, she's not had her bromide yet.'

* * *

Despite the building's outward appearance, Munro had envisaged the office on the fourth floor as a bastion of cutting-edge technology teaming with dedicated officers intent on solving the most heinous of crimes. To the contrary, he counted six empty desks, two steel filing cabinets, a broken water-cooler and three seemingly discarded laptops. The windows, coated in years of grime thrown up from the road below, afforded him a magnificent view of a discount supermarket and the adjoining car park, used, it seemed, for the sole purpose of dumping shopping trolleys, mattresses and other items of unwanted furniture.

'Is this it?' he said, turning to Cameron with a look of disdain, 'is this where you actually work?'

'Aye, it's not much to look at but it's what we call home.'

'If it was my home, I'd have it condemned,' came a voice from beyond the water-cooler.

Munro, befuddled, watched in amusement as a large, rotund figure clutching a screwdriver rolled out from beneath one of the desks and staggered to his feet.

'D.C.I. George Elliot,' he panted, beads of sweat peppering his balding head, 'can you believe it? They'll not even send an electrician up here. That's the second fuse blown in as many days.'

'I've blown a few myself,' said Munro, grinning. 'This is Charlie. Detective Sergeant Charlotte West.'

'Welcome aboard, Charlie. Before we go any further, James, I'd like to offer my condolences.'

'Very kind, I'm sure.'

'And just for the record, although I never worked with him, I'm sure Alexander wouldnae want anyone else on this but you.'

'Aye, maybe so,' said Munro, 'maybe so. Anyway, I'm happy to lend a hand in whatever…'

'Lend a hand?' said Elliot with a thunderous laugh, 'No, no, James! You're not here to lend a hand, we need every man we can get. As you can see, we're not exactly blessed with an abundance of staff. Everything's sorted, you have all the authority you need to lead this investigation and as for you Charlie, you're on the payroll for as long as it takes, is that understood?'

'Sir.'

'Good, then let's get started.'

'Just a moment,' said Munro, 'do you mean to say you're not involved in this case?'

Elliot plonked himself on the edge of a desk and regarded Munro with a tilt of the head.

'James,' he said, dabbing his forehead with a handkerchief, 'unfortunately I only have three other officers available and between us we have one armed robbery, a handful of break-ins and an outbreak of synthetic marijuana to deal with. Of course, if you'd rather swap places, I'd be more than happy...'

'Fair enough,' said Munro with a smirk, 'fair enough. Okay then, as you say, let's get...'

'Hold on, chief,' said Cameron, 'just one more introduction to make. Dougal!'

A fresh-faced lad in his mid-twenties wearing jeans, a lumberjack shirt and an expression which suggested he'd lost his pet hamster to a feral cat, poked his head out from behind one of the filing cabinets.

'Sir?'

'This is Detective Constable Dougal McCrae,' said Cameron, 'the only other string to our bow. Couldnae punch his way out of a paper bag but what he lacks in brawn he makes up for with his brain. Puts me to shame and he's half my age.'

'Is that a compliment?' said Dougal, shaking his head. 'Okay, so, who's for tea and who's for coffee?'

'Tea please,' said Munro, 'white, three sugars, and use blue top. They can skim my pay for a pension but I'll not have them do it to my milk.'

Munro stood by the window, hands clasped behind his back, and gazed down at the street below as Cameron tossed a file on the desk, fired up a laptop and eased himself into a chair.

'Okay,' he said with a sombre sigh, 'you'll forgive me if some of this sounds like I'm stating the obvious, chief, but for everyone's benefit, here it is. Agnes Craig. Single. Age twenty-two. Full-time student at Ayrshire College...'

'What was she studying?' said Munro, without turning.

'Counselling, HNC. She was in her second year.'

'Just like her father. Good for her.'

'She also worked two evenings a week and Saturdays in the bookies on Smith Street. Last seen Friday evening at The West Kirk on Sandgate where she spent the night with her best friend.'

'Sorry,' said West, 'The West Kirk?'

'It's a pub, Charlie, in an old church. Cheap and cheerful, which is why it's so popular with the students.'

'Okay, and you're sure of that? I mean, that she was there?'

'Oh aye, we've CCTV of her and her friend, they had a great time by the looks of it, apart from the odd interruption.'

'Interruption?'

'Just some neds trying to chat them up but they were having none of it.'

'Anyone stand out?' said West. 'Anyone that could have...'

'No, we've been through the footage, no-one to give us cause for concern.'

'Okay. And this friend of hers?'

'Mary Campbell. She's on the same course as Agnes and they worked together at the bookies.'

'Flatmates?'

'No, Agnes lived alone. When she failed to show for work the following day and didnae answer her phone, Mary assumed she had a hangover so went and knocked her door. The last thing she needed was to lose her job. That's when she called the police.'

'Who was first on scene?' said Munro.

'Uniform, chief. Dougal followed up. By the time I got there, forensics were in full swing.'

'Have they given you an approximate time of...'

'Aye, between midnight and 2am, or thereabouts.'

'And do we know where she went after they left the pub?' said Munro.

'Better than that,' said Cameron, stabbing a key on the laptop, 'here's the footage from the street camera. Allow me to introduce you to our prime suspect.'

'Suspect?' said Munro as he eagerly pulled his spectacles from his pocket and sat next to West.

'Okay,' said Cameron, 'this camera is directly opposite the pub. There's Agnes, see. She gives her friend a wee hug goodbye and heads north along Sandgate. Then here, look, she crosses St. John Street and careers into this fella. Forgive me for saying so, but she was blootered.'

'Can you zoom in?' said West.

'Looks innocent enough,' said Munro, squinting at the screen, 'they're laughing.'

'Did they know each other?' said West. 'Boyfriend, maybe?'

'No, I don't think so,' said Cameron, 'Mary's adamant young Agnes was well and truly single and she wasnae into one-night stands. Now watch, they head off together and turn down Cathcart Street.'

'That's where she lives?'

'Aye, and that's where we lose her.'

'Dammit,' said West, 'doesn't make things any easier for us.'

'Hold on,' said Cameron, as he fast-forwarded the recording, 'all is not lost, look. Here's our man, back again, he continues north along Sandgate then crosses the bridge.'

'And where does he go from there?' said West.

'We've no idea,' said Dougal as he set a tray on the table, 'there's no camera over the bridge so I'm afraid that's the end of the trail. However, I think we can assume if he's heading in that direction at that time of night, that he lives over that way. Tea up.'

'I'm impressed,' said Munro.

'Thanks, sir. I do my best.'

'I meant the tea, young man. China cups and a pot.'

'Oh,' said Dougal, 'well, as my mammy says, you cannae beat a brew made with leaves. My advice is to stay clear of teabags, there's no telling what's in them, despite what it says on the box.'

'A man after my own heart,' said Munro with a satisfied grin, 'you'll go far, laddie, trust me, you'll go far. Even farther if you've an oatcake or two. We've not had breakfast, you understand.'

'Sorry, sir, but it's maybe not a bad thing.'

'What do you mean?'

'I'll let Sergeant Cameron explain. When he's ready.'

Munro frowned and turned his attention to the computer.

'Have you managed to pull any stills off the recording, Don?' he said, sipping his tea, 'anything we can use to identify this fellow?'

'Ahead of you there, chief. See here,' said Cameron, pulling up a handful images, 'not bad, eh? They were used in an appeal for witnesses just this morning. Not accusing him of anything, just the usual "give us a call for a wee chat so we can eliminate you etcetera, etcetera."'

'Very good. Any response?'

'Not just yet, it's too early but I'm confident there will be.'

'Good,' said Munro draining his cup, 'so, what's next?'

Cameron glanced furtively at West as he pulled a wodge of photographs from the file and laid them face down on the desk.

'Are you ready for this, chief?' he said, almost embarrassed. 'What I mean is, I'm afraid it's not very pleasant to look at and you do have a personal connection with…'

'Och, I appreciate your concern,' said Munro, 'but trust me, there's little I've not seen before. What was it now? A stabbing? Dodgy tablets perhaps?'

'I'm afraid it's not as straightforward as that.'

'What do you mean?'

'Her heart gave out.'

'Are you joking me?' said Munro, surprised. 'A young girl like Agnes? Fit and healthy, in the prime of her…'

'I know,' said Cameron, 'it beggars belief but in the words of the pathologist, she was… she was literally scared to death. She was so petrified she had a cardiac.'

Munro glanced at West and loosened his tie.

'Okay,' he said, placing his hands palm down on the desk as if bracing himself for the news, 'let's have it.'

Cameron cleared his throat, turned over the first photograph and slid it slowly across the table. Munro stared at the image of the body sprawled out across the bed – the skirt up around the waist, the head covered by the down-turned sheet – and swallowed hard.

'Was she…?' he said, removing his spectacles, 'tied up like that, was she…?'

'No, no,' said Cameron reassuringly. 'No, sir. She wasn't. In fact, she wasnae touched. Doesnae appear to be anything sexual about the attack at all.'

'Nothing sexual?' said Munro glowering at Cameron, his lip curling in disgust. 'Nothing sexual? Listen to me, whoever did this got his kicks from tying her up and watching her struggle. That, in my book, is sexual.'

'Sir.'

'Why the sheet over her face? Dinnae tell me he did that as a mark of respect?'

West flinched as Cameron turned over the second photo, identical to the first but with the sheet pulled back. She watched as Munro silently stood and walked to the window, his jaw twitching as he ground his teeth.

'I've read about this,' he said, turning around and pointing at the print, 'this kind of twisted behaviour. It's a perverse form of humiliation often perpetrated by a misogynist, someone with a grudge against the female of the species, someone who suffers from a psychological imbalance more often than not relating to something that occurred early in their childhood.'

'James, I know it's upsetting,' said West, 'but I'm not sure I understand. What part of this is the humiliation? The tying her up? The...'

'For God's sake, Charlie, look at her! Her face, her entire mouth covered in lipstick, it's like some Freudian...'

'Chief,' said Cameron, as he took a deep breath and turned over the third photo, a close-up of Agnes's face, 'it's not lipstick...'

Munro hesitated, reached for his glasses and picked up the print.

'...it's blood.'

Chapter 5

Lizzie Paton relished her role as a receptionist – the lack of responsibility and predictability of each working day suited her lackadaisical demeanour though in reality, with only two GCSEs to her name, it was the only job she could get which didn't involve wearing an over-sized uniform, stacking shelves or serving fried chicken to leering inebriates on their way home from the pub. She was undeniably content. Content to smile inanely at the house-hunters who wandered through the door boasting about the size of their deposits. Content to spend her day flicking through the pages of Hello magazine or trawling the internet for snippets of celebrity gossip. And content to return home at precisely 5:50pm every evening to a home-made supper prepared by her mother, after which her contentment would often turn to resentment.

Life outside the office not a picture of domesticated bliss – the house was small and over-crowded, she yearned for privacy and a room of her own; but most of all, she craved company when she went to bed at night. Not that she was short of admirers. As an attractive twenty-four-year-old she'd been wined and dined on many occasions but, for reasons she failed to comprehend, not one single suitor deemed her worthy of a second date.

She gazed through the rain-spattered window at Max sitting on a pavement bench, his collar turned up against the drizzle, his nose buried deep in a book as thick as a brick, and smiled. She wanted to be angry with him but, try as she might, she couldn't. Instead, she wondered just how wet he'd have to get before he ventured inside. The flash of lightning didn't faze him. The clap of thunder exactly one and a half seconds later made him jump from his seat.

'Alright, Lizzie?' he said, tousling his sodden hair. 'What's up with you? You've a face like a bulldog chewing a wasp.'

'I'm fizzin'.'

'Why? Has someone... oh, hold on, is this something to do with me?'

'No.'

'Really?'

'Just thought you'd call, that's all,' said Lizzie, trying her best to sound upset.

'I got tied up. Look, I'm sorry, okay? I told you, I met a pal, had a few too many. Took the whole weekend to sleep it off.'

'Is that so?'

'Aye, that's so. Look, what is this?' said Max, scowling as he tossed his book on the desk. 'We're not married, you know? If you want an argument, get yourself a husband.'

'I just thought...'

'Word of advice, Lizzie – it's better to be with no-one than the wrong one.'

Lizzie gawped at Max like a scolded child.

'And I'm the wrong one, am I?' she said, forlornly.

'I don't know. Maybe. Look, I'm just being straight with you. Things are a wee bit... difficult for me right now. Okay?'

'Aye. Okay.'

'Oh, for God's sake,' said Max, tugging at his damp sleeves in an effort to remove his jacket, 'you're impossible, you know that? Look, if it makes you happy, we'll go out. How about tonight?'

'What?'

'Tonight! A wee bevvy after work, see how we go.'

'I don't… I'm not sure I can,' said Lizzie, flustered.

'Are you joking me? After everything you've just said… I give up, really. I…'

'I just don't think I can get a babysitter in time! It's short notice.'

Max froze, gave up on his jacket and slumped in his chair.

'Babysitter?' he said quietly, his eyes narrowing as he glared at her. 'Now, why… oh, I get it, you've a wee sister needs looking after.'

'No,' said Lizzie, fiddling with a pen, 'I've a… I've a wee bairn.'

'What?'

'A bairn! There, now you know. Och, let's just forget it. Who'd want to go out with a single mother anyway?'

Max sat back and folded his arms. A wry grin crossed his face.

'You,' he said, playfully wagging a finger in her direction, 'are a dark horse. What's his name?'

Lizzie glanced up and smiled.

'Her name,' she said. 'Her name is Maggie.'

'Maggie. That's pretty. Does she look like you?'

'My mammy seems to think so.'

'Then she must be a bonnie, wee lass.'

'Stop it,' said Lizzie, blushing, 'you're embarrassing me.'

'And the daddy?'

'Dinnae go there. Bastard took himself off soon as he found out I was pregnant.'

'Sorry.'

'Don't be,' said Lizzie, 'as you said, it's better to be with no-one than the wrong one.'

Max smiled.

'Okay, Lizzie, listen up,' he said as he made for the door, 'as usual, there's nothing going on here so I'm away up the bank, it's pay-day and I want to see if I've enough to get that Maserati I've my eye on. While I'm gone, you need to sort out a sitter for Friday. Got that?'

'Friday? You mean…? Aye okay, great!' said Lizzie, grinning. 'Just one thing before you go…'

'What's that?'

'Did you happen see the telly this morning? I mean, before you left?'

'Telly?' said Max, laughing. 'I dinnae have a telly, Lizzie.'

'You don't have a…? Okay, well, what about the paper then? Did you have look at the newspaper?'

'Certainly not. They're filthy and riddled with germs, besides, all news is bad news.'

'You may be right there.'

'Is there something you're not telling me?'

Lizzie passed him the newspaper.

'I… I just thought this looked a bit like you.'

Max frowned as he studied the grainy black and white images taken from a CCTV camera of a couple standing by a wall, the street light giving the figures a cold, ethereal glow.

'You're not wrong, there,' he said, 'he does look like me, even has a similar coat. What's this all about then?'

'Some girl gone missing, I think. They want to have a wee chat with that fella.'

'He must be guilty then, when the police say they want to have a wee chat, what they really mean is… hold on, it says here these pictures were taken on Sandgate. On Friday night. It is me! Look at that, Lizzie, I'm famous!'

'Sandgate?' said Lizzie, 'What were you doing on Sandgate? On Friday? With a girl? I thought you said…'

'Hey! You're not my wife, hen!' said Max, raising his voice. 'Listen, for the record, I was away off home after meeting my pal when that lassie almost fell over she was that drunk. I walked her back to her flat, that's all.'

'Oh.'

'Oh indeed. So, will I give them a call do you think? The police? Will they send a car to come pick me up?'

'Aye, of course they will,' said Lizzie, brusquely, 'do wonders for your image too, being carted off in a cop car.'

'Good point. I'll wander over instead, after the bank, see what they want.'

'Are you… are you okay?'

'Lizzie, it's another excuse to leave the office. I couldnae be better.'

* * *

The ominous silence took Dougal back to the classroom and the interminable dread he experienced as he waited for his teacher to dole out a suitable punishment for his petty misdemeanours. He sat, suppressing the urge to clear away the tray lest it should disturb Munro who stood stock-still, gazing at the thickening cloud as the rain lashed against the window. West glanced at her watch, seven minutes, she decided, was ample time for him to come to terms with what he'd seen.

'James,' she said softly, 'we need to move on.'

Munro turned and gently smiled.

'Quite right, Charlie,' he said as Dougal grabbed the tray and made a bee-line for the kitchen, 'we must move on. So, Don, what else have you got?'

'There's not much more I can tell you, chief,' said Cameron, 'we should have the results from forensics and the post-mortem any time now, apart from that…'

'Okay then. The footage. From the camera on the street. Let's see it again.'

Munro pulled on his spectacles, placed a notebook on the desk and sat, pencil poised above the page as he watched the recording.

'Stop,' he barked, hastily scribbling something down. 'Go. Fast forward, and... stop.'

Cameron looked at West and shrugged his shoulders as Munro sat back, pulled off his glasses and rubbed his eyes.

'This fellow,' he said, 'your prime suspect.'

'Aye?' said Cameron. 'What of him?'

'He didnae do it.'

'What?' said Cameron, astonished. 'Are you serious? With all due respect, chief, he's the only...'

Munro held up his hand.

'See here, Don, I'm not here to criticise, I'm here to deal with the facts, and the fact is your suspect disappears down Cathcart Street with Agnes at precisely 00:47 and 43 seconds. He re-appears at 01:02 and 12 seconds. That's not even fifteen minutes. Now, unless he holds the world record for something akin to skinning a cat, do you really think...?'

Cameron surrendered his hands.

'Stupid,' he said, shaking his head, 'I didnae even think to check the time, I just assumed...'

'Never mind that now,' said Munro. 'So Charlie, if this chap is back on Sandgate on his way home at two minutes past one, what else does that tell us?'

West stared blankly into space as she pondered the question before directing her answer at Cameron.

'You said she was killed between midnight and two...' she said.

'Aye, that's what the...'

'...well, now we know different. Obviously she was killed sometime after 1am, a window of just under an hour which should make our job looking for the perpetrator marginally easier.'

'Well done, Charlie,' said Munro. 'So, Don, Agnes's flat, is it clear?'

'Aye, chief,' said Cameron, 'do you want to...?'

'In a moment, we've just time for a wee quiz before we go.'

'A quiz?'

'Aye, something to lift the spirits. Constable, this should be easy for an intelligent, young officer like yourself.'

'Okay,' said Dougal, eager to impress, 'I like answering questions, fire away.'

'If I said E.T.D., what would you say?'

'Estimated Time of Death, sir.'

'Very good. Now, if I said R.T.C., what would you say?'

'Road Traffic Collision, sir. This is easy.'

'Is it? Okay, try this then; if I said B.L.T…'

'B… you've lost me, sir, I've never heard of a…'

'Bacon, lettuce and tomato, laddie. A popular sandwich filling often served between two slices of toasted bread and in the absence of breakfast, we need a couple up here, right away. White bread, brown sauce. Thank you.'

Chapter 6

Even without the aid of sirens or flashing blue lights, and despite the fact that he had to negotiate a one-way traffic system in the middle of a deluge worthy of the title "monsoon", it took Cameron less than ten minutes to make the journey from the police office to Cathcart Street. He parked opposite the flat and donned a baseball cap in preparation for the dash across the street.

'Okay?' he said, hand on door.

'Hold on, I need to get my bearings first,' said Munro as he pointed through the windscreen towards the top of the street. 'Up there, that's Sandgate, correct?'

'That's right, chief.'

'And the distance from there to here is what? A hundred yards?'

'Aye,' said Cameron, 'about that.'

'A minute's walk.'

'Two or three, if you've had a few bevvies.'

'Good. And to the rear of us,' said Munro, opening the window and adjusting the wing mirror, 'is Fort Street which runs parallel to Sandgate.'

'Correct.'

'Okay. Look behind you and tell me what you see, Don, just there, by the junction.'

'I'm not sure what you mean, chief,' said Cameron, swivelling in his seat, 'is it the bus stop you're referring to?'

'No, no. Next to it.'

'Sorry, chief, you've lost me, there's nothing there but a lamp post.'

'By jiminy, he's got it! Only thing is, it's not a lamp post, is it Don? It's a camera. Did you not get the footage from yon camera?'

Cameron faced front and scratched the back of his head.

'Well, no, I mean, it's not relevant, is it?' he said. 'I mean, it's pointing down Fort Street, not here.'

'Right enough, but it would still pick up any vehicle coming in this direction, would it not? I'm not here to hold your hand D.S. Cameron,' said Munro tersely, as he stepped from the car, 'if you're not up to the job, just say so.'

Cameron turned to West and cringed as the door slammed.

'What?' he said. 'It's a wee oversight, that's all.'

'I'd get that footage if I were you Don,' said West with a wink, 'or life won't be worth living.'

Cameron scurried across the street, hopped gingerly down the steps and joined an irate Munro by the front door.

'As you can see, chief,' he said, puffing, 'there's no sign of a forced entry, so it's safe to say the perp either had a set of keys or was known to young Agnes.'

'Or,' said West mischievously, 'he's an expert locksmith.'

'What?'

'A professional, someone rather adept at picking locks.'

'I never... aye, I suppose, but no, no, the chances of that would have to be...'

'Don,' said Munro, impatiently, 'if it's all the same with you, I'd prefer it if you concluded your wee tête-à-tête on the topic of housebreaking indoors. I'm getting wet. And I'm not happy when I'm wet.'

Munro pushed open the door, pulled back his hood and unzipped his coat as he peered down the dimly lit hallway.

'Is there another way in,' he said, snapping on a pair of latex gloves, 'a door round the back, perhaps?'

'There is a door, chief, leads to a small patio garden but you cannae reach it from the other side. This is the only way in and out. Lounge – first room on the right.'

* * *

Munro stood in the centre of the room, hands behind his back, and slowly turned 360 degrees absorbing every last detail, from the books on sociology, counselling and psychotherapy that lined the shelves to the Eddi Reader CD lying on top the stereo and the two distinct water rings on the coffee table. His eyes came to rest on a framed photograph hanging above the mantle shelf.

'Is that him?' said West, noticing the melancholy look on Munro's face.

'Alex? Aye, that's him.'

'He's got a kind face. Happy looking.'

'He was that, Charlie. Nothing ground the fellow down, nothing but the… Don, I take it nothing's been moved?'

'No, chief. Well, obviously a few bits and bobs are away down the lab, but apart from that…'

Munro craned his neck and stared up at the ceiling rose.

'Neighbours,' he said, 'upstairs in particular. Did they hear anything?'

'No. There's an only old fella upstairs, Bob McCluskey. He's partially deaf, wears a hearing aid and his eyesight's not too good either. He's usually in his pit by 9pm.'

'How very convenient,' said Munro, turning his attention to the window and the view from the basement up to street level, 'and next door? I assume you have done a door to door?'

Cameron glanced at West, stuttering as he answered.

'Yes chief, well… what I mean is, no, not the whole street, just the immediate neighbours. I've spoken with the folk just next door, same response. No-one's seen or heard anything.'

The ensuing silence caused Cameron to shuffle nervously on his feet.

'Are you okay, chief?' he said. 'You're, er, you're not saying much. Is something up?'

Munro flexed his shoulders and slowly turned to face Cameron, his cold, blue eyes fixing him with a penetrating gaze.

'Aye, Don,' he said, his voice low and menacing, 'something very big is up. A young lassie is bound hand and foot to her own bed, in her own home and she has her lips ceremoniously sliced from her face. Now, do you not think she would have said something? Screamed just a wee bit, perhaps?'

Cameron swallowed hard, his throat as dry as a bone.

'Aye chief, of course, but like I said, the neighbours…'

'Perhaps,' said West, with a timely interruption, 'perhaps she was drugged.'

'That is a possibility Charlie,' said Munro without averting his gaze, 'but we shall have to wait for the results of the post-mortem before we can pursue that. It's also possible she may have expired before being tied to the bed. Possible, but I dare say unlikely. Don, bedroom?'

'Down the hall, chief, follow me.'

Cameron stood to one side and watched as Munro slowly scoured the room from top to bottom. The bed was stripped to the mattress. The dry shampoo, can of deodorant, bottle of perfume, tin of lip balm, hair brush, comb and toiletry bag were all perfectly aligned atop the chest of drawers. The two books, one of poetry and a novel, were placed neatly on the bedside table next to an alarm clock and reading lamp. A dressing gown hung behind the door and the slippers, side by side, were tucked just beneath the bed. The room was as neat as a pin with OCD. He moved to the window and pulled back the net curtain with his forefinger.

'Tell me, Don, is there anything about this room that troubles you?' he said, admiring the collection of pot plants outside.

'No, chief,' said Cameron, 'in fact I'd say it was really quite pleasant, not that I've seen many bedrooms but…'

'Take another look. Take another look and tell me if there's not something a wee bit… unsettling about the place.'

'Unsettling?' said Cameron as he looked at West and shrugged his shoulders.

'Come on, come on, no conferring, clock's ticking. No? Och, too bad, out of time. Charlie, bonus points for a correct answer.'

'It's too clean,' said West. 'Too neat. Too tidy. In a word, there's no sign of a struggle.'

'Correct. No sign of a struggle, which tells us…?'

'She went to her bed willingly. Who knows, maybe she thought something a little bit "kinky" might be fun or… or she was out cold and placed there.'

'I favour the latter,' said Munro. 'Agnes, I can assure you, was not the kind of girl to do "kinky". So, next. The deranged delinquent responsible for this atrocity tied her feet using a hairdryer and a phone charger but her hands were bound with cable ties. Why? They're not the kind of items one would normally have about one's person.'

'Good point,' said West, 'so maybe he used them professionally, you know, like if he was an electrician or a builder, then he could have had a few in his pocket.'

'That's exactly what I was thinking,' said Cameron enthusiastically, 'see, I'm with you on this, Charlie. If Agnes was having some work done, you know, some wiring or something, even just getting a quote, then it could have been someone she was familiar with, someone who came back and…'

'Or perhaps they belonged to Agnes in the first place,' said Munro, gazing outside, 'I dare say there's a bagful somewhere, kitchen drawer no doubt.'

'Kitchen drawer?' said West. 'What would Agnes be doing with a…'

'Securing her plants to a stake. Like yon rosebush by the wall there. The ties outside are exactly the same as the ones in the photographs, are they not, Don?'

Cameron fumbled for his phone and headed for the door, head bowed.

'If it's all the same with you, chief,' he said groaning with embarrassment, 'I cannae get a signal here and I have to make a couple of calls, chase those test results and arrange to get the film from that street camera. I'll be in the car.'

'Did you have to be so harsh?' said West as the front door slammed, 'he's obviously trying his best and they are under-manned up here. He's stressed out, you can tell by the bags under his eyes.'

'Och, Charlie, you know me well enough, lassie, I'm not after persecuting the man but can you not see something's troubling him? He cannae concentrate and it's interfering with his police work. Something's amiss, Charlie, trust me. Something's amiss.'

* * *

Dougal McCrae was not typical of his generation. He had no interest in football, horse racing or online poker, baulked at the idea of sitting in a darkened auditorium watching the latest blockbuster next to somebody intent on devouring an extra-large bucket of popcorn and would rather spend his weekends fishing for brown trout in Loch Doon than recovering from a hangover.

Inquisitive by nature, he could have pursued a successful career in engineering or medicine but such vocations were limited in their scope insomuch as the problems he'd encounter could eventually be solved by assigning one of many pre-existing answers. As a detective, however, such multiple-choice solutions did not exist, thereby affording him the opportunity to sate his appetite for discovering the unknown.

Tucked away in the corner of the office, he sat hunched over his computer and scowled at the screen as the sound of the door opening interrupted his train of thought. Munro turned to West, pressed a finger to his lips and listened, the only sound that of somebody tapping furiously on a keyboard.

'Dougal. Is that you?' he said.

'Sir,' came the disgruntled reply as Dougal, sighing, peered out from behind a filing cabinet.

'It's awful quiet in here, are we interrupting you?'

'No, you're alright, sir, I prefer it quiet, helps me concentrate when I'm working.'

'I see,' said Munro, 'and what exactly are you working on?'

'Background check, sir.'

'Background check? Anyone we know or is it someone you intend having a wee drink with this evening?'

'Andrew Maxwell Stewart, sir.'

'That's a fine name Dougal,' said Munro, shaking the rain from his jacket and draping it over the back of a chair, 'but if it's not too rude a question, who exactly might he be?'

'He's the fella downstairs, sir,' said Dougal, 'in the interview room.'

'Sorry Dougal but see, when it comes to crosswords, I tend to avoid the cryptic clues.'

'Oh Christ! Sorry, I mean, I should've said, he's been waiting for you. He's the fella on the camera with Agnes, you know, the one we've been appealing for.'

'I see, and he just…'

'Aye, just walked in, seems keen to help.'

'And how long has he been here?'

'Since ten o'clock, at least. I have to say, he's been awful patient.'

'Good, well he's obviously in no great to hurry to leave, which gives us time for another quiz.'

'Another quiz?' said Dougal, rising to the challenge.

'Aye. Charlie here is flustered by a particularly troublesome conundrum, her ability to think somewhat impaired as a result of having not eaten for several hours. Perhaps you can help.'

'Okay, I'll do my best.'

'Good, see if you can complete this sequence: Breakfast. Brunch. Lunch…'

'Tea!'

'Excellent idea Dougal. White, three sugars and while you're at it, see if you can rustle up something edible for Charlie, the poor lassie's on the verge of keeling over. Then go fetch Mr. Stewart from the interview room, there's really no need for him to be languishing down there on his own.'

Chapter 7

West, fearful that somebody else might enter the room and deny her the opportunity of devouring the fifth and final finger of shortbread, whipped it from the plate and moaned ecstatically as her blood sugar levels began to rise while Munro gently sipped his tea and scribbled a list of tasks for Dougal to attend to.

'It's getting late,' he said, laying down his pen, 'we should consider heading back as soon as we've spoken with Mr. Stewart.'

'Okay,' said West, 'rain's eased off, shouldn't take long. I'll drive if you like.'

'Good. We'll stop by the butcher on the way and pick something up for supper, something a wee bit more substantial than a plateful of…'

He paused as Cameron, looking exhausted, slipped through the door, raised his eyebrows in greeting and sat quietly at the opposite desk. He dragged his laptop towards him and pulled a flash drive from his pocket.

'Are you okay, Don?' said Munro. 'You seem a wee bit…'

'Just the traffic, chief,' said Cameron curtly, 'rush hour, it's nose to tail on the bridge and that numpty at the council office, he's more interested in clocking off than helping the police with a murder inquiry. Jobsworths, the lot of them, it's always a struggle trying to get anything…'

'Couldn't they have emailed you the footage from the camera?' said West. 'Surely that would have saved you…'

'You've not had much dealings with the bureaucrats in office, have you Charlie? Would've taken another three days by the time they got around to processing the request, rubber-stamping it in triplicate and… och sorry, look, I didnae mean to snap, I'm just feeling a bit…'

Cameron closed his laptop without bothering to finish his sentence as Dougal returned with Max in tow.

'Ah, Mr. Stewart I presume?' said Munro with a welcoming smile, 'come in, take a seat, had we known you were here we'd have come back sooner. It's decent of you to wait so long.'

'Nae bother,' said Max, 'you're the police, you must be busy all the time.'

'Aye, right enough. Are you not staying Don?' said a concerned Munro as Cameron rose from his desk and buttoned his coat.

'No, no. If it's all the same with you, chief, I need to shoot off, my head's…'

'On you go then, we'll fill you in tomorrow. So, Mr. Stewart…'

'Max. I'm not one for formalities.'

'Max it is. I'm James, Detective Inspector James Munro and this young lady is Detective Sergeant West. Now, I trust you've been well looked after? Refreshments and such like?'

'Aye. Very kind, thanks.'

'Good. Tell me, Max, before we go on, Detective Constable McCrae says you've been here all day, I'm not one to pry but do you not have any work to do?'

Max raised the corner of his mouth and shook his head, smirking.

'I've a job, if that's what you mean. It pays a wage which means I can pay the rent but it's about as interesting as watching a cup final.'

'You've obviously not seen Celtic play. What is it you do exactly?'

'Sell houses. Well, I would if I had any to sell.'

'Estate agent, eh?' said West. 'Must be tough when you have to rely on commission to make a living. Anyway, back to business, what can we do for you?'

'What can you do for me? It's the other way around, is it not?' said Max, pulling the folded newspaper from his pocket and handing it over. 'My friend, I mean the girl I work with, Lizzie, she gave me this, this morning, so I came right over.'

Munro unfurled the paper and looked at the photographs.

'Och, they're not very flattering are they?' he said. 'I could do better with a Box Brownie.'

'A what?'

'Never mind,' said Munro. 'So, would you like to tell us what happened? With this lassie you met?'

'We didnae meet exactly, collided more like. She crashed into me, hammered she was. Her name's Ness, said she'd been down the West Kirk with a friend. Obviously made a night of it.'

'Well, Friday night,' said West, 'can't blame her for that. How was she?'

'Blootered,' said Max.

'I mean, did she seem anxious, upset, depressed?'

'No, no, she was flying, happy as Larry.'

'What did you talk about?'

'Talk about? Bugger all, she could hardly string two words together. If you dinnae mind me asking, what's this all about? Has something happened to her?'

'You could say that,' said West, 'I'm afraid Agnes has been…'

'Agnes,' said Munro, interrupting, 'has passed on.'

46

'Passed on?' said Max, bewildered, 'you mean dead?'

'Aye, to be blunt. Dead.'

'But she was so… I mean, Jesus. Mortality, eh? One minute you're here, the next… how? How did she…?'

'That's what we're trying to find out,' said West, 'so, can we just go back a bit, what took you to Sandgate in the first place?'

'I often go,' said Max, 'by way of a constitutional, like. After my supper.'

'I'm guilty of that myself,' said Munro, 'I like to walk off a meal. Do you remember what you had?'

'Haddock. I always have haddock on a Friday and a Tuesday. Steak on a Saturday and a Wednesday, and chicken on Sundays and Thursdays.'

'And Mondays?'

'Vegetables. Baked potato mainly.'

'You like your routine then?' said Munro.

'Aye. I do that.'

'Any particular reason?' said West, 'I mean, for adopting such a regimented approach to dining?'

Max regarded her as though it were one of the stupidest questions he'd ever heard.

'No. I just do it. It's just the way I am.'

'Fair enough. I wish I could be that organised, it'd certainly make shopping a darn site easier. So, you finished your supper. Then what?'

Max, sitting with his back straight, knees together and hands folded in his lap, looked to the ceiling with a gentle frown.

'I put the wrappers in a blue, plastic carrier bag,' he said, 'tied it with a knot and tossed it in the bin. Then I put an empty beer can in the sink, fetched my coat and left.'

'And where do you stay, Max?' said Munro. 'Is it nearby?'

'Aye. Main Street, it's not far from here.'

'Go on.'

'Well, as I say, I left the house, headed out over the bridge and then down Sandgate. It takes approximately nine minutes and thirty seconds to reach St. John Street. I normally go further but my walk was curtailed on account of the, er, the collision.'

Munro nodded, encouraging Max to continue.

'She could hardly stand so I offered to call her a taxi. She laughed cos her house was just around the corner so I said I'd walk her home instead. Cathcart Street. Third house from the end. Basement flat. 7C. Black front door. Silver letterbox. There's no latch on the gate from the street.'

Munro, enthralled by the clarity of Max's recollection, leaned forward and regarded him with an admiring smile.

'You've a memory for detail, Max,' he said, 'in fact I'd say it was quite remarkable. Aye, that's the word. Remarkable. Tell me, do you recall anything else about the walk back? To her flat, that is. Anything at all?'

'Oh aye,' said Max, 'we passed two fellas, they laughed like they were embarrassed for me, must've have thought we were an item. Both about six feet tall, short hair, dark. One wearing a turtle neck, the other a cardigan over a polo shirt.'

'Can you hold on a minute please Max,' said West as she grabbed the laptop and played back the footage, 'I just need to… okay, go on.'

'You dinnae believe me, do you?' said Max, 'that's why you're looking at that film.'

'I believe you implicitly, Max, but I do have to verify…'

'Okay, stop it there, I'll tell you what happens next then you can see if I'm lying or not.'

West huffed indignantly and paused the film as Munro, entertained by the challenge, grinned in anticipation of the impending duel.

'Okay,' said West, 'so, what happens next?'

'Just as we get to the corner, there's a blue BMW, five door saloon, 3-series, I think, pulls out of Cathcart Street and does a right down Sandgate.'

'Very good,' said West, sarcastically.

'And then a fella runs by, from behind, cannae say why but he's wearing a cagoule, black with silver piping.'

Munro sat back, folded his arms and smiled contentedly.

'I'm not easily impressed, Max,' he said, 'but I have to say... are you not of a mind to enter a game show or two? You could fair wipe the board with a memory like yours.'

'Me?' said Max, laughing, 'you're joking, right?'

'But you're obviously very clever, I mean, your ability to...'

'I'm not clever, Mr. Munro. I havenae got a single qualification to my name, not even a GCSE.'

'You left school early then?'

'You could say that. I was asked to leave. No, actually, that's not strictly true, they told me to leave.'

'Because?'

'Take your pick: unruly behaviour, disruptive influence, inability to concentrate...'

West did not believe in magic and she was sceptical of illusionists but as Max was neither, there was something about his ability to recall events in such detail that unnerved her. She leaned back, hand on chin and regarded him curiously, flinching visibly, as he caught her staring, his eyes as black as coal.

'So,' she said, flustered by his unwavering gaze, 'you saw Agnes to her door, that's her full name by the way, Agnes Craig, and then...'

'And then she invited me in. She offered me a wee drink as a thank you for seeing her home safe. I wasnae keen on the idea but...'

'Why not?' said West, 'I mean, why weren't you keen? Most men...'

'I'm not most men, Miss West. I'm not… I'm just not very good in the company of women.'

'That's alright, if you're…'

'No, I'm not. I'm not gay if that's what you're implying. I'm just not very good in the company of women.'

'Sorry, I didn't mean to… so you went in, albeit reluctantly?'

'Aye.'

'And does your incredible memory stretch to the interior of her flat?' said West, cynically.

Max glowered at West and paused to lick his lips before answering.

'Beige carpet,' he said as his eyes narrowed. 'Beige carpet, white walls, cream-coloured curtains and sofa. Coffee table: wooden. Framed photo of a man and a girl above the fireplace. Stereo with CD player…'

'I think we've got the picture, Max,' said West, clearing her throat, 'and did you have that drink or…'

'Sip. I had a sip of a drink. It was vodka. Neat. Smirnoff. She was dozing on the sofa so I left. I set the glass on the table and I left.'

West, her face a subtle shade of blush, closed the laptop and turned to Max.

'Well,' she said, forcing a smile, 'I think that's everything for…'

'Hold on, miss,' said Dougal, 'if I may, I've a wee question for Max.'

'Fire away, Mr. McCrae,' said Max, 'if I can answer, I will.'

'Thank you. What time did you leave the flat?'

'It was one minute after midnight.'

'And you went straight home?'

'I did that.'

'And did you notice anything when you left,' said Dougal, 'what I mean is, anything out of the ordinary?'

'That depends on your definition of ordinary, Mr. McCrae,' said Max, 'but I did notice the curtains twitching in the flat above. Someone watched me leave.'

'The flat above? So, that would be the flat at street level?'

'Aye, right enough. Whoever lives there thought they were invisible but you cannae spy on folk in you've a lamp glowing in the room.'

'That's great. Anything else?'

'No. Oh, three cars parked outside.'

'And why would that be unusual?' said Dougal.

'Because the street was near enough empty but these three were almost, kind of, sandwiched together.'

'I don't suppose you…'

'Two silver: a Polo and a Micra, and one white. A Corsa.'

Munro stood up, rubbed his hands together and grinned at Max.

'I cannae thank you enough for coming by to see us, Max,' he said, 'you've been incredibly helpful. Really you have. Now, I'll not keep you much longer, just a couple of things before you go. You're not obliged in any way but…'

'I ken what you're saying, Mr. Munro. It'll help eliminate me from your inquiry.'

'Aye, something like that. A few details that's all, address, place of work and, well if you dinnae mind, fingerprints would be the icing on the cake.'

'No problem. Will we do it now?'

'Aye,' said Dougal, 'top man. Come with me and…'

'No, no,' said Munro, 'Charlie, would you take Max downstairs. I need to run through this list with Dougal then we can all be off.'

Munro waited until the door had closed before turning to Dougal who sat motionless, his face overcome with a look of dread.

'What is it, Dougal?' said Munro. 'You look as though you're going to the gallows.'

'Sorry, it's just that whenever somebody says they want a word or…'

'Och, grow up, laddie. If I was going to berate you I'd not be doing it with a smile on my face, I can assure you of that. Now, that background check on young Max there, did you find anything?'

'No, sir,' said Dougal with a sigh of relief, 'nothing at all.'

'You mean he's clean?'

'No, I mean I couldnae find anything. He's not on any social media, you know, Facebook or Twitter, and there's no profile of him anywhere else, previous employers, clubs, that kind of thing. If it wasn't for the council records he'd be near enough invisible.'

'I see,' said Munro, 'tell me… I mean, you must be of a similar age, does that not strike you as odd?'

'Aye. Well, no. Unusual perhaps, but not everyone wants to put their life story online.'

'Fair enough. Okay, there's a few things I need you to do for me tomorrow morning; first of all, nip over to Cathcart Street and have a word with the fellow who lives upstairs. I want to know if he saw anything.'

'Okay, but has D.S. Cameron not done that already?'

'Never mind what D.S. Cameron has or hasnae done, Dougal. Just do it.'

'Sir.'

'Then see if you can trace the owners of the vehicles Max mentioned, see if they live nearby. Finally, do some digging on Agnes's friends and work colleagues, see if anyone's been hounding her or taken an unhealthy interest in her activities.'

'Right you are, sir. You think maybe she's rubbed somebody up the wrong way?'

'No, no, I doubt that very much. Young Agnes was as popular as a Tunnock's Teacake at a marshmallow convention. I'm just wondering if she'd managed to get herself a stalker perhaps.'

'Nae bother. Is that it?'

'No,' said Munro, as he perched on the edge of the desk and lowered his voice, 'no, it is not. I need to ask you something else. In confidence. If you feel you cannae answer, then I'll respect that and we'll say no more.'

'Sounds serious, sir. What is it?'

'Don. D.S. Cameron. Is he... is he alright?'

'How'd you mean?' said Dougal.

'Well, I'm not that familiar with the fellow but his behaviour seems a little...'

'Unpredictable? Lacking focus?'

'Aye, Dougal, that's it. Exactly.'

'I thought the same. I mean, he's a good cop, sir, there's no denying it, but I think...'

'What Dougal?' said Munro. 'What do you think?'

'Between you and me, sir, I think he came back too early. After the incident.'

'The incident?'

'Aye. You must've seen the scar by his eye. Well, that's not the only one. He's a fair few across his body. Armed robbery it was. Attempted armed robbery.'

'Go on.'

'He was off duty, went to grab a few tinnies from the off-licence when some ned thought grabbing the money from the till would be easier than signing-on or getting a job. D.S. Cameron intervened but the fella was a nutter. Went berserk. Spent three and a half hours in hospital getting stitched up. Missed an artery by a whisker. Doctors said he shouldnae be back for at least another month.'

'I never realised. And this was recently?'

'Recent enough,' said Dougal, 'he was meant to see a therapist to help him get over the trauma but he jacked it in before it started. Said it wouldnae do him any good. Said being a cop was the same as falling off a bike, you get knocked off, you get straight back on again.'

Munro walked to the window and looked out across a darkening sky.

'I don't mind telling you,' he said, 'I'm a wee bit concerned. Concerned he may become a liability and jeopardise the investigation. Is there anything else I should know?'

'Aye, maybe. Och, I'm not sure if it's my place to say anything, sir. I mean, it's a wee bit… personal.'

'It's entirely up to you laddie. I'll not hold it against you if you feel like you're betraying a trust.'

Dougal ruffled his hair and sighed as he toyed with his conscience.

'His wife,' he said, 'his wife left him.'

'Ah.'

'While he was in hospital.'

'Oh.'

'She went to see him once they'd patched him up. Fair ranting she was, said she'd had enough of being married to a copper. Apparently.'

'Apparently?'

'Like I said, sir, it's not for me to comment on other folks' domestic situations.'

'And what about the fellow who attacked him? Did you…?'

'Clean away, sir. Not a trace. Can I go now?'

'Aye,' said Munro, 'thanks Dougal. See you in the morning.'

* * *

Munro returned to the window, the view nothing more than his own ghostly reflection, straightened his tie and contemplated the consequences of keeping Cameron on the team as the door opened behind him.

'All done,' said West, sounding deflated. 'You ready?'

'Aye,' said Munro, hesitating as he reached for his jacket, 'I've just a… a wee niggling sensation, that's all.'

'About Max?'

'No, no. Don. I want you to keep an eye on him.'

'Why?' said West.

'Let's just say he's some personal issues to deal with,' said Munro. 'Personal issues that may be clouding his judgement. I'll explain on the way but I cannae afford to carry him if he slips up again.'

'Again?'

'First the missing film from a camera pointing at the scene and now, if we're to believe what young Max has told us, lying about interviewing the neighbours.'

'You mean the bloke in the flat above?' said West.

'That's exactly who I mean.'

'Well there is another side to that, you know. Don may well have questioned the old bloke but he might've said he was in bed because he didn't want to get involved.'

'Maybe,' said Munro, 'all the same, I'm sending Dougal to see him tomorrow, then we'll know for sure.'

'Okay. Can we go now?'

'Aye, we can. Incidentally, what did you make of Max?' said Munro, pulling on his jacket.

'Max?'

'I imagine he's feeling a wee bit... raw, wouldn't you say?'

'Raw?'

'Aye. Your interview technique, Charlie. It was as abrasive as sandpaper.'

'Oh come off it,' said West, 'I was just pushing him, wanted to see if he was legit and not trying to pull the wool over our...'

'The poor chappie came to help,' said Munro, 'of his own free will, and all you did was...'

'Well, I don't trust him. He's smart. The kind of bloke that'll lead you down a path to nowhere.'

'Is that so?' said Munro, his face breaking into a grin.

'He's got that look.'

'And is that a look of guilt? Or the kind of look that makes him attractive to the opposite sex?'

'Ha, bloody ha. Come on, I'm starving. How about I make us some spaghetti when we get back?'

'Charlie, I'd rather navigate the Limpopo in a coracle than eat a plate of pasta. I'll fetch a steak on the way.'

* * *

Max, irritated by the fact that his routine had been adversely altered, ambled along the deserted, rain-sodden streets, past the shops long closed for the day and struggled to convince himself that a vegetarian Chinese take-away was a viable substitute for a baked potato laden with baked beans and cheese. He stopped outside the bookies and checked his phone. Three missed calls. Lizzie Paton.

'Sorry, we're closing,' said a petite blonde as she pulled the door behind her, 'manager's locking up.'

'What?' said Max. 'You can't be, you have to stay open until the last race…'

'The last race has been and gone,' she said. 'Windsor finished at eight and Hamilton was abandoned.'

'No matter,' said Max, 'I'm not interested in the races, I just want to lose a few quid in one of those machines of yours, it'll only take a minute.'

'Sorry, mister, nothing I can do.'

'Och, come on, give us a break here, I've had a pig of a day.'

'Haven't we all.'

'Look, I've not had my supper, I've spent all day with the police and my routine is completely out of kilter, I need to…'

'Police?' said the girl, stepping back. 'What were you doing with the police?'

'Och look, I've not done anything if that's what you think, I was just helping them with…'

'Oh aye. Helping them with what?'

'If you must know,' said Max, 'some lassie who got… I mean, I walked her home and now she's…'

'Who? What lassie?' said the girl.

'For Christ's sake, what is this? Look, Friday night, right, this girl crashed in to me, totally hammered, so I walked her home and now she's…'

'Dead.'

'Aye. Dead. But how did you know?'

'What was her name?'

'What? What's it to you?'

'I said, what was her name?'

'Agnes,' said Max, 'Agnes Craig. Are you okay? You've gone awfully pale. Oh no, don't tell me you knew…?'

The girl froze. She stood, fists clenched by her side and stared at Max, her eyes wide with rage, before erupting in a fireball of fury.

'What did you do to her?' she screamed. 'What did you…?'

'Hold on!' said Max, holding up his hands as he backed away, 'I didnae touch her! I walked her home, that's all. I promise, I didnae touch her!'

'You bastard!'

'I didnae touch her! All I did was…'

The sound of the shutter as it creaked and groaned towards the ground drowned out his voice. By the time it hit the pavement with a satisfying thud, the girl's screaming had turned to sobbing, her shoulders quivering uncontrollably. She slowly raised her head and looked at Max.

'Sorry,' she said, 'I'm just… I'm still…'

'Aye, understandably so,' said Max, keeping his distance, 'listen, if it helps, if you need to punch somebody, feel free, I can take it.'

The girl spluttered as she laughed.

'Thanks,' she said, wiping her face with the cuff of her sleeve, 'so you… you were the last person to see Agnes alive?'

Max frowned.

'Well no, that's not strictly true, there must have been at least one other…' he said, grimacing as he realised what he'd said, 'shit, that didn't come out the way it was meant to, I meant…'

'It's okay,' said the girl. 'I know what you meant. So, did you know her?'

'No, no. Like I said, I just saw her home safe and sound. Only she wasn't, was she? Safe, I mean.'

'It's not your fault, you did the right thing. So, do you have a name?'

'Max. Andrew Maxwell Stewart. But folk call me Max.'

'Mary Campbell.'

'Mary Campbell? *"She has my heart, she has my hand, By sacred troth and honour's band! Till the mortal stroke shall lay me low, Im thine, my Highland Lassie, O!*'

'What's that?'

'Och, just something I remember from school, it was written for a lassie called Mary. I think. Oh, hold on, no, I may be confusing it with…'

'Doesnae matter, look, I should be…'

'Listen, I was thinking…' said Max, 'I mean, I'm not very good at this but… I need a drink. Would you…?'

'No thanks. Not being rude but I need to go, I've a friend coming at nine.'

Max paused.

'A friend? Wee bit late for callers, is it not? Must be a male friend.'

'None of your business,' said Mary, smiling, 'but if you must know, it's a lady friend, she's a teacher and she's simply dropping off a few bits and bobs to help me with my coursework. Alright?'

'Aye, alright. All the more reason to make sure you get there in one piece. Have you far to go?'

'Queens Terrace.'

'By the beach?' said Max.

'Aye.'

'Must be nice.'

'It has its moments,' said Mary.

'Okay, well, we best get going.'

'I've told you, I'm a grown woman, I think I can take care of myself.'

'I've no doubt you can, Mary Campbell, but you're still in shock and it's late. Come on, I insist.'

Chapter 8

Unlike Munro, who preferred to watch the sun rise rather than set, West, being more owl than lark, favoured lingering beneath the duvet for as long as possible, advocating the most productive time of day as the hours between nightfall and 6am when the chances of being distracted by alcohol, television or a lamb biryani were minimised.

Despite the early start she still managed, however, to bag herself an extra hour's sleep by snuggling up on the capacious back seat of the ageing Peugeot as Munro chauffeured her up to Ayr. She awoke only when he returned from the café, aroused by the aroma of freshly-brewed coffee and toasted bacon sandwiches.

'You're a star,' she said, crawling to the front seat.

'Hands off,' said Munro, as he tucked the bag beneath his seat, 'you can wait like the rest of us.'

* * *

Cameron was at his desk, engrossed in what appeared to be a lengthy letter embellished with a fancy logo at the head of each page. He jumped as Munro and West entered the office, scrambling to tuck the letter back into the envelope.

'Don!' said Munro cheerfully. 'Nice to see you here so early.'

'Nae bother, chief, it's a damn site easier for me than it is for you, I'm only up the road.'

'Nonetheless, dedication reaps its own rewards. Speaking of which, as the catering here cannae stretch to anything more than a bowl of cereal or a sandwich that curls instinctively at the edges, you'll be pleased to know I've taken it upon myself to ensure our calorific intake is enough to avoid unnecessary bouts of dizziness or amnesia. Help yourself. Where's Dougal?'

'Been and gone, chief,' said Cameron, reaching for a coffee, 'he's away down the college, gone to have a chat with Agnes's classmates.'

'I see. Oh well,' said Munro, plucking a toastie from the bag, 'another one for you then, Charlie. So, Don, have we any news?'

'We have, chief. Results came in last night, forensics and post-mortem, it makes for interesting reading. Grab a seat and I'll…'

'No, no, I'm away just now. I need a word with George. Go through it with Charlie and you can feed me the salient points when I get back. I'll not be long.'

* * *

West threw her coat over the back of a chair, unwrapped a sandwich and sat opposite Cameron.

'So,' she said with a smile, 'how're you feeling today?'

'Feeling? Okay. Why?' said Cameron defensively.

'No reason. Just that yesterday you seemed a little, I don't know, preoccupied, a bit…'

'Aye,' said Cameron, 'sorry about that. I shouldnae bring my problems to work, it's not very professional and to tell the truth, I've not been sleeping great either.'

'Wouldn't worry. Bad news then?' said West, nodding at the envelope on the desk.

'You're familiar with the phrase "it never rains, it pours"?'

'Story of my life.'

'Well, I'm in for a proper drenching.'

'Want to talk about it?'

'With you?' said Cameron. 'I'd rather not, it's personal and the fewer folk who…'

'Suit yourself,' said West, yanking the lid from a coffee cup, 'so, these results, what have they found?'

Cameron picked up the envelope, folded it in half and rammed it into his trouser pocket before opening the laptop.

'Okay,' he said, 'let's do forensics first. Here we are. It's the wife.'

'Pardon me?' said West.

'My wife. She's instigated divorce proceedings. That's the letter.'

'Oh. Sorry. Are you…?'

'Surprised? Upset? Totally and utterly pissed off? Yes to all of the above.'

'And there's… I mean, there's no chance of a reconciliation?'

'No.'

'Oh well,' said West. 'Tell me to mind own business if you want but was it… you know, another bloke?'

Cameron sniggered.

'In a manner of speaking,' he said.

'So is that where she's gone?'

'No idea. But I'd say she's probably stopping with that nutter of a sister of hers.'

'Nutter?'

'Aye, she's not right in the head,' said Cameron, 'took a shine to me first time we met and she's been after me ever since.'

'You should be flattered, I suppose.'

'You're joking me, she's no spring chicken, if you ken what I'm saying.'

'I see,' said West, rattled by the chauvinistic remark, 'and does your wife know how she feels about you?'

'She thinks it's "sweet", funny even, makes my skin crawl.'

'A case of unrequited love, eh?' said West. 'Oh well, at least you know where to find her if you want to try and patch things up.'

'Oh no,' said Cameron, sniggering. 'You'll not find me knocking her door, cap in hand, I'd rather… what am I doing? I said I wasnae going to talk about it.'

'Helps though, doesn't it? Talking, I mean,' said West, eyeing him curiously. 'What's up? You wouldn't be wincing like that over a letter.'

'Nothing gets past you, does it?' said Cameron.

'Not much.'

'Forgot my painkillers. My shoulder's a wee bit…'

'Hold on,' said West, reaching for her bag, 'I've got some paracetamol here, they should help. By the way, you should wipe your hands on a napkin, not your tee-shirt, that's probably bacon fat, it'll stain.'

'I haven't… och, that's not bacon fat, Charlie, that's where… it's taking time to heal, weeps a bit now and then.'

'What does? What weeps?'

'Och, it's just a scratch,' said Cameron, 'I tried to stop some numpty robbing the off-licence a while back, unfortunately he had a knife and I didn't.'

'Is that how you…' said West, pointing to his eye.

'Aye. Same fella, same knife.'

'Right, come on,' said West, 'shirt off, let's clean that up before we do anything else. First aid kit?'

'Filing cabinet. Bottom drawer.'

West, with the remainder of her sandwich gripped firmly between her teeth, grabbed a box of sterile wipes and a roll of sticking plaster from the box and turned to face Cameron who sat, head bowed, naked from the waist up.

'Bloody hell!' she said, almost choking. 'A scratch you said, you look more like a bloody dartboard! How many…'

'Nine,' said Cameron, 'it's not as bad as it looks, they're not very deep.'

'You,' said West, scowling, 'shouldn't even be here, no wonder your head's in the bloody clouds.'

'Oh aye, and what else would I do with my time? Dinnae fret, Charlie, I'm fine. Really, I am.'

'Well you'd better be,' said West as she dressed the wound, 'because, and I'm giving you the heads up here, if Munro doesn't reckon you're up to it, he'll have you off the…'

'Aye okay, I figured that out for myself already. So, shall we get on? Results?'

* * *

George Elliot was not afraid of danger. Blessed as he was with an abundance of height and girth, the very sight of him was enough to deter many a miscreant from perpetrating a crime. As a young officer he'd acquired his fair share of accolades and a reputation amongst his peers for being fearless in the face of adversity but, with the passage of time, he'd grown to favour an approach to policing which involved utilising his brain rather than his fists, thereby ensuring a degree of longevity to his existence.

He checked his watch and grumbled impatiently, shifting uncomfortably in his seat as he grew increasingly frustrated with the millions of results Google had thrown at him.

'Aye, what is it?' he said gruffly as a short, sharp rap on the door interrupted his browsing.

'George,' said Munro, as he entered the room, 'is this a good time?'

'James! Couldnae be better, come in, sit down. Now tell me, what do you give somebody as a 30th wedding anniversary gift?'

'Oh, a medal I'd say.'

Elliot slumped back and laughed out loud.

'Just the tonic, James. Just the tonic.'

'Am I right in thinking congratulations are in order?'

'Aye,' said Elliot, 'but if I dinnae get my act together, there'll not be a 31st.'

'Well, it shouldnae be hard. A 30th anniversary is pearl.'

'Pearl? That's great, something else I cannae afford. What did you do, James? Did you give pearls?'

'No, no,' said Munro, 'I bought Jean a wetsuit and told her to dive for them herself.'

'I like your style, James,' said Elliot, grinning, 'certainly be a lot cheaper.'

'Well if money's an issue, why not treat her to champagne and oysters?'

'Allergic to seafood.'

'I see, well just the champagne then. It'll have much the same effect as the oysters, after a glass or two, that is. When is it?'

'Tomorrow.'

'In that case,' said Munro with a wink, 'I'd forget the pearls altogether and start looking at hotels if I were you, and the farther south the better.'

'You're a genius. You think maybe somewhere like... Wales, perhaps? Or Cornwall?'

No, no, keep going and dinnae stop till you hit Tenerife, at the very least.'

'Oh, God. So, what's up? Is this a social call or...'

'It's an "or". D.S. Cameron.'

'Don?' said Elliot. 'What's up?'

'I understand he was involved in a wee incident recently.'

'Och, you mean the hold-up? Aye, he should've kept his nose out but there's no telling some people?'

'How do you mean?'

'Don can be a wee bit... headstrong. Bull in a china shop, if you ken what I'm saying.'

'Aye, typical Taurean,' said Munro. 'I wonder, was he... was he passed fit for work before returning?'

'I believe so, why? Is there a problem?'

'No, nothing major, not yet. He just seems… unsettled, depressed, even. I'll keep an eye on him, of course, but if there's anything you can…'

'Not really, James,' said Elliot, 'it's probably down to a lack of rest, after all, it was quite an ordeal by all accounts.'

'So I hear.'

'Hefty fella too. He was lucky to get away so lightly by the sounds of it.'

'And no arrests were made?' said Munro.

'No. We did have a couple of leads, early on, but they fizzled out.'

'Och well, let's just hope he's not one for vigilante justice.'

'Don? No, he may be headstrong but he plays by the rules.'

'Fair enough,' said Munro. 'Unfortunate state of affairs all the same. Aye, that's the word. Unfortunate.'

* * *

Upon his return Munro was both surprised and delighted to find the atmosphere in the office akin to that of a library, though, with the remnants of breakfast still strewn across the desks, not as clean. West, head in hands as she studiously leafed through the forensics report, glanced up momentarily.

'Alright?' she said. 'Come and sit down, you're not gonna like this.'

'Tea, chief?' said Cameron as Munro pulled up a chair.

'Aye, that would be most welcome, thanks Don. So, Charlie, what have we got?'

'Right, forensics first. I'll keep it brief. Two tumblers were taken from the lounge, both dusted for prints. One set belongs to Agnes, the other, we now know, belongs to Max.'

'Okay,' said Munro, 'that's to be expected. What else?'

'Max's tumbler tested positive for vodka, no surprise as it had hardly been touched but Agnes's tested positive for vodka and… ketamine.'

'Ketamine?' said Munro.

'Aye, chief,' said Cameron, handing him his tea. 'Ecstasy, sort of, just not your usual kind.'

'A rogue batch you mean?'

'No, no, it was kosher alright but the amount present in the vodka didnae come from a tablet. The ketamine was administered in liquid form.'

'I see. And we know that because?'

'A tab wouldnae dissolve.'

'And the liquid form, is that easily available?' said Munro, 'or is it a prescription drug?'

'Chief,' said Cameron, smirking, 'these days you can get anything you want without a prescription.'

'Aye, right enough,' said Munro, 'so, it looks as though you were right, Charlie – she was drugged before being moved to the bedroom. Top marks. Go on.'

West looked blankly at Munro and shrugged her shoulders.

'What?' he said. 'You mean that's it?'

'Fraid so,' said West, raising her eyebrows. 'Incredible, isn't it? But that's all they could find. Whoever did this knew how to cover their tracks. The only prints in the entire flat that didn't belong to Agnes, belonged to Max, and the only place they appear is on that glass.'

'Astounding,' said Munro as he sat back, 'truly astounding.'

'I know. Not even a whiff of a smudge on the front door.'

'Footprints?'

'Fully carpeted.'

Munro stood up, glanced first at West, then at Cameron, picked up the mug of tea and paced slowly around the room.

'Let's move on,' he said impatiently, draining his mug as he returned to the desk, 'post-mortem.'

'Post-mortem. Right,' said Cameron, clearing his throat, 'I should warn you, chief, it's not very… entertaining.'

Munro, staring at the floor, elbows on knees and hands clasped before him, said nothing.

'Okay, I'll start with the, er… the facial injuries: two clean cuts, no snagging or tearing. The instrument was small and razor sharp, probably a surgical blade. Based on the depth of the flesh at the site of the intrusion and the lack of scarring to the gums or teeth, they estimate the size of the blade to be a 10 or 11. Cuts were made from left to right suggesting the assailant was right-handed and there is no evidence of any further trauma to the body, i.e. no bruising or cuts, apart from the abrasions to the wrists and ankles as a result of being bound to the bed.'

Munro raised his hand, causing Cameron to pause.

'This weapon,' he said quietly, without looking up, 'a scalpel. Why use such an instrument of precision when – fact – most attacks of this nature are executed by an aspiring butcher with a knife of outrageous proportions? What does that tell us? Don, just for the record, Charlie's winning 1-0, you're playing catch-up.'

'I… I suppose he could be in the medical…'

'Och, Don, come, come, why? Because he used a scalpel? No, no, you can buy the blessed things in any art and craft shop. No, it's because…'

'It's because,' said West, 'he knew exactly what he was going to do and he had to be quick which means this wasn't impulsive; the attack was premeditated so, that being the case, he probably didn't choose his victim at random. He'd probably been stalking her.'

'2-0. Go on, Don.'

Cameron glanced furtively at West and took a deep breath before continuing.

'Traces of ketamine were present in the stomach and bloods,' he said, 'proof conclusive that…'

'That she was killed by an overdose?' said Munro.

'I'm afraid not, chief,' said Cameron, hesitating, 'the ketamine wasnae enough to knock her out, it made her delirious, yes, but…'

'So what you're saying is…'

'Aye. I'm afraid she was… she was conscious the whole time.'

'Dear God.'

'Actual C.O.D. was heart failure. She was literally scared to death.'

Munro stood abruptly.

'Excuse me, just a moment,' he said, leaving the room, 'I'll not be long.'

Cameron and West locked eyes and sat silently gazing at each other, neither daring to speak until Munro returned a few minutes later, dabbing the corner of his mouth with a handkerchief.

'Apologies,' he said, 'I had something in my eye, had to flush it out. So, Don, is there anything else we should be aware of?'

'No, chief,' said Cameron, 'if you've any questions the fella to contact is a Dr. Kelly.'

'At the Queen Elizabeth? In Glasgow?'

'No, he's head of pathology here in Ayr. Agnes's body is back now awaiting funeral arrangements.'

'Okay,' said Munro, 'I think we'll have a wee chat and there's no time like the present. Charlie, you with me. Don, I want you to call Dougal, find out where he is. If he's not finished at the college, get yourself over to the bookies and have a word with anyone there who knew Agnes. I want to know everything, no matter how minor it may seem. I want to know if they socialised, where they went, what they talked about, including the gossip. Got it?'

Chapter 9

Even as a single mother living in the parental home with a job that paid little more than the minimum wage, Lizzie refused to see her glass as half empty. Instead, she embraced motherhood, was thankful to be in gainful employment and eternally grateful that she had found in her own mother not just a child minder but arguably her best friend.

Despite the recurring pangs of loneliness, experienced more often than not at night, she was indomitably cheerful and generous to a fault, though her most endearing trait was the fact that she completely underestimated, without being self-deprecating, just how attractive she really was. Even Max who, purely because of his lack of experience with women, had avoided developing an intimate relationship with anyone, couldn't help but warm to her.

'Looks like someone got the cream,' he said as he arrived for work.

'No,' said Lizzie, beaming, 'just glad it's Tuesday.'

'Really? Tuesday? Why's that then?'

'Because it means there's only two more days till Friday.'

'And Friday's important, why?'

'Are you joking me?'

'Aye,' said Max, 'and you fell for it. So, what's it to be? Pub? Restaurant? Library?'

'Library?'

'Why not? Listen, hen, if you want to see how much you have in common with someone else, you can do worse than browse a bookshelf or two together.'

The smile dropped from Lizzie's face as she lowered her head.

'I'm not really one for reading,' she said, almost embarrassed.

'Nae bother,' said Max, 'we can look at the picture books instead.'

'You've a cheek. So, come on then, tell me, how'd it go?'

'How did what go?'

'Only the most exciting thing that's happened to you in the past month. The police.'

'Oh, that,' said Max, 'aye, it was alright, no big deal. Spent the day hanging around waiting for them to show up, they asked a few questions, I gave them some answers and that was that.'

'Really? And there was I thinking they'd have you tied to a chair, shining spotlights in your face and threatening to send you down for life.'

'Wishful thinking.'

'I did call, you know, just in case.'

'Aye, I see that, thanks, but it was late and I had to get my supper. Coffee?'

'You havenae time.'

'Lizzie,' said Max, laughing, 'if there's one thing I have in spades, it's time.'

'Not today, you haven't. That bungalow on Ashgrove Street, you've a viewing in twenty minutes.'

'What?'

'They seem quite keen. Och, come on, smile. At least it gives you something to do.'

71

* * *

Max, having trudged begrudgingly across town, spied the eager couple hovering outside the property grinning like a pair of newly-weds and approached them sporting the most insincere grin he could muster.

'Hello,' he said, 'you've come to view the house?'

'That's right,' said the lady, clinging to her husband's arm, 'it looks perfect and we've a mortgage sorted already.'

Max rubbed his chin and grimaced like a plumber about to give an estimate.

'Well, sorry to burst your bubble, madam,' he said, 'but it's gone.'

'Gone?' said the man despondently, 'but how? There's another two weeks until the bids close.'

'Bids? No, no. It was changed to fixed price,' said Max, lying through his teeth, 'did they not tell you?'

'What? No. When? How much do they want?'

'Doesnae matter,' said Max, 'as I say, it's gone. You folks have a nice day now.'

The couple watched despairingly as he turned on his heels and set-off at a brisk pace in the direction of Waterstone's.

* * *

The manageress, leaning on the counter with her head resting on her hand, glanced up from her inventory as Max breezed through the door, plucked a copy of Marcus Aurelius's *Meditations* from the shelf and, unaware of her gaze, settled into his usual chair. She watched as he eagerly opened the book and smiled softly to herself, fascinated that someone so young could find philosophy so absorbing. Forty-five minutes later she glided over and settled silently beside him.

'How's it going?' she said, her voice a husky whisper, 'the search, I mean.'

Max dog-eared the right-hand page, closed the book and turned to face her, perturbed by the glint in her eye.

'Not that good, actually,' he said.

'Same here,' said the manageress, 'there was somebody once, took a couple of years to realise it but in the end, well, I suppose we just didnae click.'

'Aye, you and a few million others. No doubt you were predictably upset?'

'Predictably? Are you inferring that women are emotionally more vulnerable than men?'

'No. What I'm saying is you have to look at it from another perspective. Loss is nothing but change, and change is Nature's delight.'

The manageress, sporting a wry grin, said nothing.

'What?' said Max, intimidated by her seductive stare. 'What's the problem?'

'No problem,' she said, 'I'm just trying to figure out if you're cynical, angry or just plain cold towards the opposite sex.'

'Neither. I'm cautious. See, everything in the universe happens for a reason, every tiny action has a direct consequence on a pattern of events. There's no room for impulsiveness.'

'In that case,' said the manageress, 'I fear the quest for your other half may never reach a satisfactory conclusion.'

'Meaning?'

'Well, I'm no expert but based on the world's population I imagine it's fair to assume we'd probably have to "experience" hundreds of potential matches before we find the missing piece of the jigsaw.'

'Aye, right enough. Maybe.'

'Then surely by exercising caution you're diminishing your chances of success by narrowing the field.'

'Oh aye?' said Max, turning away and opening the book. 'And you'd rather play the field, I suppose?'

'Naughty,' said the manageress, her forefinger nestling between her lips, 'I just have a feeling you and I might…'

'No, no. I dinnae think so,' said Max, dismissively, 'not being rude but I cannae see it happening somehow.'

'What's your number?'

'Come again?'

'Your number. In case you change your mind. I'll ring and hang up then you'll have me as a missed call. Hopefully not a missed opportunity.'

Max puffed out his cheeks with a sigh.

'Okay,' he said reluctantly, 'go on. What name will I put?'

'Jeannie.'

* * *

Although its appearance had more in common with a budget hotel perched beside a motorway than a pioneering hospital, the pervasive aroma of Iodoform was irritatingly familiar. Munro's nose twitched disapprovingly as they approached the visitor desk where a polite, middle-aged lady in a navy-blue blazer offered them a sympathetic smile in a manner befitting that of an undertaker.

'Hello,' she said with a tilt of the head, 'how can I help?'

'Dr. Kelly, please,' said West, waving her warrant card.

'Is he expecting you?'

'No.'

'Not to worry,' said the receptionist, nodding towards the bank of vacant chairs, 'you have yourselves a seat and I'll see if I can find him for you.'

West watched from the corner of her eye as an impatient Munro stared blankly out across the car park and tapped his foot to a frenetic jazz beat that only he could hear.

'You still hate hospitals, don't you?' she said, trying not laugh. 'Same as last time, you can't wait to get out.'

'Nothing's changed, lassie,' said Munro, 'so far as I'm concerned, a hospital's nothing more than the boarding gate on your trip to the other side. And, incidentally, all the tickets are one-way. Now, if I'm not mistaken, here comes one of the cabin crew.'

A tall, wiry man with a mop of spindly, red hair and a complexion as wan as a cadaver padded towards them, an over-sized tweed jacket flapping loosely from his shoulders.

'Doctor Kelly,' he said, proffering a bony hand, 'What can I do for you?'

'Detective Inspector Munro and this is Detective Sergeant West. It's about Agnes Craig, are you familiar…'

'Och, quite familiar Inspector, but if I may be so bold, if it's about the Craig lassie, should I not be talking to that Cameron fellow? I thought he was…'

'I'm leading the investigation, Doctor Kelly. D.S. Cameron is a part of my team.'

'I see,' said Kelly, 'well, not that it matters. Are you here to view the body or is it the funeral you've come about?'

'Neither,' said Munro as they all sat, 'I'm curious about some aspects of her death, are you okay to talk?'

'Aye,' said Kelly, 'I'm in no rush.'

'Good. First of all, the cause of death – we've established that as heart failure, correct?'

'Loosely speaking. Myocardial infarction to be precise.'

'Heart attack?' said West.

'Indeed. In this instance, caused by the narrowing of the arteries as a result of the copious amounts of ketamine in her system. That coupled with the ordeal she went through, well, her heart simply couldn't cope.'

'This ketamine,' said Munro, 'it wasn't your usual recreational drug, like ecstasy, was it? I mean, she didnae take a tablet, did she? It was a liquid.'

'Ketamine hydrochloride,' said Kelly, 'incredibly strong, incredibly toxic and, if taken with alcohol, well, the consequences would indeed be fatal. Not a nice way to go.'

'Can you be more specific?' said Munro.

'Repetitive bouts of vomiting, loss of vision, dizziness, palpitations, high blood pressure, hallucinations…'

'Okay, I think we've got the picture,' said West. 'What's it used for, Doctor Kelly? As a liquid? I mean, is it that common?'

'Oh aye, very common in the right environment.'

'Like hospitals?'

'Aye, like hospitals. It's used mainly as an anaesthesia and for pain management too, for example as a substitute for morphine. Oh, and there was some marginal success in its use to treat depression as well but the results weren't conclusive enough to prove it beneficial although, having said that, there are those who self-medicate.'

'And this ketamine hydrochloride,' said Munro, 'is it readily available? Could you get it with a prescription, for example?'

'No, no,' said Kelly, 'well, certainly not on the NHS. If you're trying to trace a source, my advice would be to check with all the veterinary surgeons in the area, see if they've had a break-in, perhaps.'

'The vets?'

'Aye, it's used on animals for the same reasons but probably more so.'

'I see. Okay, we'll do that. Thanks,' said Munro, as he stood and zipped his coat. 'Well, we've taken up enough of your time, I'm sure you've plenty to do, I appreciate your help.'

'You're welcome, Inspector,' said Kelly as he shuffled away, 'anytime, and give my best to that Cameron fellow, tell him I hope he's getting plenty of rest.'

Munro froze and glanced at West, a worrying frown creasing his brow.

'Doctor Kelly!' he yelled across the hall. 'Hold on a moment.'

Kelly stopped in his tracks, turned and ambled back towards them.

'Is there something you forgot to ask, Inspector?' he said.

'No, no,' said Munro, rubbing his chin in an effort soothe his addled mind, 'it's something you said, just now. You said to make sure Cameron was getting plenty of rest. Why is that?'

'Well, isn't it obvious?' said Kelly. 'After the affray he was involved in? The body needs time to heal, Inspector, you cannae just…'

'Hold on, hold on,' said Munro, 'you know about the attack?'

'Aye, of course, I was here when he came in. Well, over in A&E. I was covering for the usual lack of staff.'

'So you patched him up?' said West.

'I wouldnae go as far as that, miss,' said Kelly, 'my job is to open bodies, not close them up. I cleaned the wounds and left the needlecraft to somebody else.'

Munro held a hand aloft, buying time as he collected his thoughts.

'By all accounts,' he said, 'D.S. Cameron was lucky to get away so lightly. From what I've heard, his assailant was quite a hefty chap.'

'Is that so?' said Kelly, sniggering, 'Well, I've no idea who he's trying to impress but I'd find that… questionable.'

'Can you explain?' said West. 'It'd be a great help.'

'Of course. Look, if you're a big fella with a knife and you're going to stab someone, chances are you'd hold it by your side with your fingers curled upwards around the handle and stab with a forward-thrusting motion, right? Now, if you do that and you're a wee fella, you'll only end up stabbing your victim in the lower stomach, if you're lucky, so you'd hold the knife up high, like this, and bring it down, not forward, that way you can be sure of wounding the poor fella in the chest.'

'And the wounds inflicted on Cameron…'

'The angle of the wounds indicate irrefutably that he was stabbed with a downward thrusting motion thereby suggesting his assailant was considerably shorter than himself.'

'I see,' said Munro, 'but I imagine the force of the blows must have caused quite some damage then?'

'Not really, whoever attacked him wasnae very strong. A kid maybe, young teenager. It's not as though we had to put him in ICU.'

'But he was here a while?'

'Och, no more than normal for anyone in A&E,' said Kelly, 'a couple of hours, I'd say. No more than that. Once he'd had his tetanus, he was on his way.'

'Do you,' said West as she glanced knowingly at Munro, 'do you happen to remember what D.S. Cameron was wearing when he came in?'

'I get the feeling someone on your team is heading for detention Inspector. I'm right, am I not?' said Kelly, failing to illicit a response. 'Och, nae bother. Jeans, boots and a white tee-shirt. Red and white to be precise, the red being a consequence of the...'

'Jacket?'

'Leather. An old leather jacket.'

'One last question, Doctor Kelly,' said Munro as he turned for the door, beckoning West to follow, 'do you think it was the leather jacket that saved him? Did the jacket stop the knife from penetrating deeper?'

'The jacket?' said Kelly, grinning, 'Dearie me, no, no. There wasnae a mark on it. I can say quite categorically, Cameron wasnae wearing that jacket when he was attacked.'

Chapter 10

Dougal's dexterity on a keyboard and his ability to focus on more than one foe at a time was a skill honed in his bedroom where, as an adolescent, he whiled away the evening hours saving the planet from assured Armageddon by warring with all manner of alien invaders on his PlayStation. He sat, engrossed, in front of two laptops, watching both screens simultaneously as he scrutinised the footage from the camera at the end of Cathcart Street and the one on Sandgate in search of a common denominator.

'Dougal, I'm not one for hide and seek, laddie,' said Munro as he and West returned to base, 'if you want some lunch, you best show your face.'

'Lunch?' said Dougal, creeping out from a darkened corner of the office. 'Already?'

'Already?' said Munro. 'Dear, dear, some of us were up before you went to bed, laddie. Are you not familiar with the dawn chorus?'

'No, sir, sorry. Is that Elgar?'

'Never mind. If you're not hungry I'll not force you to eat but Charlie here thought you'd enjoy this – it's peri something or other which, if you dinnae mind me saying so, smells as though it's seen better days. Is D.S. Cameron back yet?'

'No, he's probably still chatting with the folk down the bookies.'

'Och, well,' said Munro, passing the remaining sandwich to West, 'looks like you've hit the jackpot in the calorie contest today, Charlie. So, Dougal, fill us in while you familiarise yourself with yon teapot.'

'Sir. As you said, Agnes was as popular as anything. Obviously, I didnae get to speak to everyone but those I did talk to wouldnae have a word said against her. Friendly, helpful, generous, smart, modest, funny. A wee bit cagey about boyfriends, relationships, that sort of thing, but…'

'What do you mean, Dougal?' said West. 'I don't follow.'

'Och, it's just something one girl said, that when they were talking about boyfriends, as lady folk tend to do, Agnes would keep quiet. I wouldnae read too much into it though, I mean, by all accounts she was quite a modest lassie, not one to brag, if you ken what I mean.'

'Okay, nice one,' said West, 'what else?'

'The cars on Cathcart Street,' said Dougal, 'the three vehicles Max mentioned. I've checked them out and they're all kosher, the owners live on the street.'

'You have been busy, well done, Dougal,' said Munro as he opened his sandwich and peered despondently at the meagre slice of processed cheddar lying beneath two wilting slices of tomato, 'I think you've near enough done a day's work already.'

'Nae bother,' said Dougal, setting down a pot of tea, 'but that's not all, I've something to show you, when you've finished your lunch, like.'

'No, no, my appetite's on the wane all of a sudden, show me what you have.'

Munro and West stood behind Dougal as he took his seat in front of the laptops.

'Okay,' he said, 'I've been whizzing through the footage from both cameras for an hour before and an hour after the estimated time of death. Now, look at this.'

'Hang on,' said West. 'How can you look at both laptops together?'

'It's not difficult, miss,' said Dougal, 'if you watch both together it's easier to spot a similarity.'

'Have you got ambidextrous vision?' said Munro.

'Is there such a thing?'

'Well, apparently so. Okay, carry on.'

'Right,' said Dougal, pointing to the laptop on his right, 'this is the film from the camera on Sandgate, as you know it's opposite the pub, about a block south of Cathcart Street. Now look, this vehicle here, tucked just behind the bus, the black saloon with the tinted windows, it comes down Sandgate and disappears around the one-way system only to reappear here, on the other camera. Then it disappears from view as it turns into Cathcart Street and reappears here, back on Sandgate, cruises south in a different lane then off it goes, around the one-way again.'

'Does he not get dizzy driving round in circles?' said Munro.

'Well, could be anything, Dougal,' said West, 'he might be lost or a mini-cab touting for business, or…'

'Hold on, miss,' said Dougal, 'here's the thing. Look at the time: 11:52pm. Agnes and Max would be somewhere on Cathcart, right?'

'Okay.'

'Now, look. Same saloon, back again, turns down Cathcart but… it doesnae reappear on Sandgate for another forty-one minutes.'

The ensuing silence was almost more than Dougal could take. Fearful he'd made a schoolboy error in his otherwise astute observations, he sat stock-still waiting for the inevitable barrage of abuse until the unexpected slap across the shoulders caused him to jump from his seat.

'Sterling work, laddie!' said Munro, 'Really, you've excelled yourself. Now tell me, have you had time to run a check on the vehicle yet?'

'Aye,' said Dougal, 'just before you came back.'

'Christ, there's no stopping you, is there?' said West with a congratulatory grin, 'well done, you.'

'I wouldnae get too excited if I were you, miss. Not just yet, anyway.'

'Ah-ha, a chink in Superman's armour.'

'The registration number. It doesnae exist.'

'Come again?'

'The car, it's a Vauxhall Astra, I've got that, but the reg, EU55 FAS, is false.'

Munro walked to the front of the desk, perched on the edge and folded his arms.

'So,' he said, smiling broadly, 'what would be the most logical thing to do next, Dougal? Assuming you're right about the make and model, that is.'

'Well, I reckon, if it was down to me, I'd contact the DVLA, get a list of all the registered Astra owners in the area and pay them a wee visit.'

'Dougal,' said Munro, 'as soon as we have a spare moment or two, it will give me great pleasure to stand you a glass or two of the finest malt we can lay our hands on. Now, any word from D.S. Cameron?'

'No, sir, not a dickie bird.'

'Why am I not surprised? Charlie, give the man a wee call, would you, tell him I want to know where the hell he is and what he's playing at.'

Munro paused as a concerned and perspiring Elliot swung through the door, a look of consternation on his face.

'George!' said Munro, 'are all the hotels booked?'

'No, no, I've not come about that.'

'Well, if you're after borrowing the wetsuit, I'm afraid I dinnae have it anymore.'

'More's the pity, James. More's the pity. There's something you need to see, right away. It's on the beach.'

Chapter 11

Were it not for the presence of the incongruous white privacy screens billowing in the breeze, the setting – with the afternoon sun bouncing off a calm sea and a clear, blue sky offering uninterrupted views across to Arran – would have been picture perfect. A handful of onlookers, intrigued by the arrival of several police officers, gathered on the esplanade to speculate on the origin of the flotsam or jetsam which lay hidden from view.

Munro took a lungful of fresh air, nudged West with his elbow and nodded in the direction of the officers milling around on the beach.

'I smell something fishy,' he said, 'and it's not coming in off the Firth.'

Cameron, catching his eye, left the group and dashed towards them.

'Don,' said Munro, 'do you have a sixth sense?'

'Sorry?'

'How did you know what was going on here?'

'Pure luck, chief,' said Cameron, buttoning his coat.

'Is that so?'

'Aye. I was at the bookies, see, talking to the manager. Seems the only other person working there today who knew Agnes was Mary Campbell, she's the lassie who found Agnes, remember?'

'Aye,' said Munro. 'And?'

'Her shift started at one o'clock so I hung around so's we could have a chat but she never showed up, so I came to her house. Uniform were already here.'

'I see. Quite a coincidence. And you're sure it's her?'

'Aye,' said Cameron, 'I'm certain.'

Munro, his eyes as cold as steel, fixed Cameron with a penetrating gaze.

'Let me tell you something, Don,' he said, menacingly, 'there's only two things in life of which you can be certain – gravity and death. And both will pull you to the ground. What's the story?'

Cameron fumbled for his notebook and flicked needlessly through the pages.

'Well, I've interviewed her flatmate,' he said, 'fella by the name of Walker. According to him, she came home last night just after half-eight, had some cheese and crackers, then a friend of hers turned up around nine. She had some bits and bobs for Mary, something to do with a college project – sketch pads, coloured pencils, arty stuff, that kind of thing.'

'And did he know this friend?' said West.

'Nope. Never seen her before.'

'Did he get her name?'

'Er, no. He left them to it. Said they went to the beach to look at the stars and have a wee natter. He got up this morning and knocked her door but there was no reply so he figured he'd let her sleep and went back an hour later. That's when he discovered her bed hadnae been slept in so he came down here.'

'So it was Walker who found her?' said West.

'Aye, he's fair shaken, understandably.'

'Aye,' said Munro, staring out to sea. 'Understandably. Where does she stay?'

'Not twenty seconds from here, chief,' said Cameron, 'Queens Terrace. Oh, one more thing, the manager at the bookies.'

'What of him?' said Munro.

'He says he saw Mary arguing with some fella on the street as he was locking up last night, then they sort of made-up and walked off together.'

'Boyfriend?'

'Unlikely,' said Cameron, 'description matches our pal Max.'

'What?' said Munro. 'Max? And you didnae think to say so earlier?'

'Well, I was coming to it, chief, I've not had the chance to…'

'See here, Don, this is what I need you to do, okay? One, get yourself back to Mary's place and check her room. See if anything turns up. Two, look out for any cameras on the way and get the footage over to Dougal by this evening. I'll give you a head start, there's one in yon car park, got that? And three, pick up Max. I want him in the office by the time we get back. Understood?'

'What's up?' said West, as Cameron disappeared from view.

'I'm really not quite sure, Charlie. Suffice to say, the last time I felt like this, they offered me beta-blockers.'

* * *

Munro, hands clasped firmly behind his back, stood motionless as he surveyed the body, beset by rigor and coated with a fine dusting of sand. Five feet, six inches in length, or thereabouts; white trainers; navy blue duffle coat buttoned to the neck with the hood up and a scarf, tweed, wrapped around the head.

'Well one thing's for sure,' he said, 'she not rolled in with the tide. First assumptions Charlie?'

'Doesn't look right,' said West, frowning as she waved a hand over the body, 'the position she's in.'

'Go on.'

'Well, it was cold last night, cold enough to wear an overcoat, so even if she'd lain down cos… I don't know, she was drunk or felt drowsy, she'd have curled up to keep warm or turned to face the wall to block out the wind.'

'Aye, she'd not be lying flat on her back with her arms by her side. Good. What else?'

'Gloves. It's cold enough for a coat and scarf, but no gloves? Doesn't add up. And one more thing – I think Don must have a sixth sense after all, I mean, how could he possibly know that this is Mary Campbell? She's wrapped up like an Egyptian mummy, I mean, come on, you can barely see her eyes let alone her face.'

Munro smiled as he snapped on a pair of gloves and crouched by the body before gently teasing the scarf from the face. Mary's eyes, dark brown and bloodshot, stared back at him.

'She didnae pass peacefully,' he said softly, 'she's a look of fear about her.'

Gripping the scarf between his thumb and forefinger, he glanced at West before taking a deep breath and, fearing the worst, pulled it tentatively down towards her chin. His shoulders slumped with a sigh of relief when he saw her mouth was intact.

'Thank Christ for that,' he whispered, pausing as he noticed the dried blood caked to the underside of the scarf.

'Let me,' said West as she knelt beside him and gently tugged it from her face, cringing at the sound of the woollen fibres as they tore themselves from the blood-encrusted wound on her neck.

'She might have screamed,' she said, 'but with no vocal cords…'

'Right enough,' said Munro, leaning in for a closer look. 'It's a clean cut, Charlie. A single, clean cut. Just like Agnes. Whoever did this knows how to handle a blade.'

'Think we've got a serial on our hands?'

'Och, come on Charlie, you should know better than that,' said Munro as he reached into one of the pockets on the duffle coat, 'apart from the fact that these two girls knew each other, there's absolutely nothing to suggest their deaths are connected in…'

Munro hesitated as he retrieved a quarter bottle of vodka from the pocket, empty bar the usual couple of drops lingering at the bottom.

'…unless, of course, this tests positive for ketamine that is. Bag it for the SOCO please, Charlie.'

* * *

Dougal, diligently monitoring the progress of the printer as it churned out the data sheets from the DVLA, allowed his mind to wander as he contemplated a weekend's fishing on the banks Loch Doon with nothing for company but the osprey and hen harriers and a Tupperware box crammed full of beef paste sandwiches. His reverie was shattered as Cameron burst through the door and glanced around the office.

'They're not here,' said Dougal.

'What? Who?'

'Munro and D.S. West, they're away down the beach.'

'I know where they are,' said Cameron angrily, 'I've just left them.'

'What was it? They left in an awful hurry, is it another…'

'I'll tell you later. What're you doing just now?'

'Finally got that info from the DVLA,' said Dougal, 'I never realised the Astra was so popular, it seems so nondescript. I've never noticed them before.'

'Och, get a life Dougal,' said Cameron, sweating, 'listen, check your inbox later, there's footage from another camera coming to you. I've an errand to run just now so that's me away. Oh, by the way, that Max fella is downstairs in the interview room. If the chief's not back in half an hour, go check on him, okay?'

'Nae bother, sir. Shall I say where you're…?'

Dougal stared at the door as it slammed shut, shrugged his shoulders and returned to collating the print-outs. He checked his watch, considered looking in on Max but thought the better of it as Munro and West, looking jaded and worn, returned from the beach.

'Dougal,' said Munro as he slumped in a chair, 'before we do anything else, is there a half decent hotel nearby? I simply cannae face the drive back tonight and Charlie here is liable to fall asleep at the wheel.'

'Aye, there's the Ayrshire and Galloway, it's not far. I'll see if they have a couple of rooms. You'll like it there, good food too. Hold on.'

West, desperate for some kind of refreshment, switched the kettle on, opened the fridge and, in the absence of any milk, turned it off again.

'Hope they've got a bloody big bar,' she said with a sigh.

'All done,' said Dougal. 'It's under your name, sir, two singles.'

'Much obliged. Now, has D.S. Cameron been back?'

'You've just missed him, sir. Said he had an errand to run and to let you know Max is downstairs waiting for you. He also said I'm to expect some more CCTV footage but didnae say what or why.'

Munro wiped his face with his hands and sighed.

'It'll be from a camera by the beach, Dougal, the car park. I'm sorry to say we've another body. Agnes's friend, Mary Campbell.'

'That's too bad,' said Dougal, 'really, I mean, who would want to do such a thing? It's not natural.'

'Agreed, laddie. Agreed. Anyway, see if you can spot anything, will you? Not now, of course. It's late, you take yourself off.'

'But what about Max? Do you need me to…?'

'No worries, Dougal, thanks,' said West, smiling appreciatively, 'we just need a quick chat concerning his whereabouts last night, won't take long, then we'll be off too.'

* * *

Max, seated with his back to the door, was trying his best to overcome an attack of the jitters. He closed his eyes, breathed deeply and concentrated all his efforts on remaining calm as he waited patiently for someone to arrive. His head twitched at the sound of the door opening.

'Apologies for calling you back so soon, Max,' said Munro as he walked around the desk, 'but we just need a quick... what in the name of God happened to you?'

Max stared blankly at Munro, then at West. A soft, nervous grin creased his face.

'You know,' he said, lowering his head, 'the first time I came here, I did so of my own accord. If you wanted to see me again, all you had to do was ask.'

'I don't follow,' said West, gazing intently at his swollen eye, half-closed due to the purple, golf ball-sized bruise to his right cheek, 'I thought D.S. Cameron was picking you up?'

'D.S. Cameron? You mean Al Pacino in the leather jacket? Oh, he came to the office, right enough. He barged through the door and before I knew what was happening, he grabbed the back of my head and slammed it into the desk, then dragged me out by my collar.'

'He did what?' said Munro, clearly agitated.

'Can anyone corroborate this?' said West.

'Aye. Lizzie. She was screaming her head off. In fact, she went ballistic, I've never seen her so angry.'

'Anyone else?'

'The boss. He's not impressed, probably thinks I'm mixed up in some gangland feud or something.'

'Okay,' said West. 'Look, I may need a statement off them at some point but in the meantime, we'll get that looked at before you go.'

'No, no, you're alright,' said Max. 'I'll survive.'

'Can I get you a drink, then? Cup of sweet tea, it'll do you good?'

'Thanks. I think I'll wait until I get home, have something a wee bit stronger.'

Munro leaned back, folded his arms and regarded Max with a look of sympathy.

'I'm shocked,' he said softly, shaking his head. 'No. Abhorred. Aye, that's the word. Abhorred. Do you want to press charges?'

'Press charges?'

'Aye. Assault.'

'But he's a police officer.'

'I dinnae care if he's the Pope,' said Munro, grinding his teeth. 'Assault's assault and this kind of behaviour is beyond reprehensible. I'll make sure you get all the help you need if you want to go ahead.'

'No,' said Max, slightly flustered. 'I mean, he'll probably come after me. I'll think about it, okay? Let me have a wee think.'

'Max,' said West as she reached for her phone, 'do you mind if I take a picture? Might come in useful, if you'd rather not, just say.'

'Nae bother, miss, go ahead, but it's not my best side, not anymore.'

Munro turned to West.

'Make sure Dougal gets that,' he said quietly, 'quick as you can.'

Max wiped his nose with the back of his hand and glanced furtively at Munro.

'Can I ask a favour?' he said.

'Of course, what is it?'

'I called Lizzie while I was waiting, told her not to worry, that everything was okay, but a wee call from yourselves to my boss wouldnae go amiss. I cannae afford to lose my job and he's bound to crucify me after this.'

'Leave it to me, Max,' said Munro. 'Rest assured, I'll speak with him in person. You'll not lose your job.'

'Thanks. So, what was it you wanted anyway?'

'Well,' said West, 'if you're up to it, just a couple of questions regarding your whereabouts last night.'

'Is that all? Christ, I thought it was something important. Okay, fire away.'

'Right, let's take it from the beginning. What did you do when you left here?'

'Let's see,' said Max as he tilted his head back and focused on the ceiling, 'I went to fetch my supper, it was late, right? But all the shops were closed. I got confused. I get confused if my routine's interrupted.'

'Remind me,' said West, 'what exactly was wrong with your routine?'

'Monday. I have to have veggies for my supper on a Monday. All I wanted was a potato and I couldnae find one. Anyways, before I knew it, I was at the bookies.'

'The bookies?' said Munro. 'I've not had you down as a gambling man, Max.'

'No, don't get me wrong, I'm not into horses or anything like that, just those glorified fruit machines. I've calculated the chances of winning are actually quite reasonable, if you know what you're doing.'

'Is that so?' said Munro, surprised. 'Tell me, Max, how much have you won exactly?'

'Nothing.'

'Och, well, maybe next time. So, you're at the bookies?'

'Aye, but they were just closing up and wouldnae let me in. I'm ashamed to say I lost it with the lassie outside, my fault entirely, I was hungry and out of sorts, I think I made her cry.'

'Heat of the moment, I expect,' said West, 'we all get stressed. What happened next?'

'Well, once we'd calmed down she told me she knew the girl who was murdered, that Agnes lassie. She was her best friend. Her name's Mary. Anyway, it was late and dark and after what happened to Agnes I felt sort of obliged to see her home, safe like. So I did.'

'You walked Mary home?' said Munro.

'Aye. Queen's Terrace. Wooden door, no number, brass letterbox and knocker. There's a window box out front, nothing in it though.'

'Do you remember what time you left her?'

'8:37pm. I waited till she'd locked the door behind her.'

'How chivalrous of you,' said West, torn between giving him a vote of sympathy and following her initial instinct and branding him guilty, 'so, time's getting on, what did you do after that?'

'Chinese,' said Max. 'Against my better judgement, I opted for a Chinese. Golden City. Spring rolls, bean sprouts and mushroom noodles. And before you ask, I was there at 8:56pm and got home at 9:27.'

'After which,' said West, 'no doubt you watched some telly and went to bed.'

Max laughed.

'I dinnae have a telly,' he said.

'You don't have a... oh, hold on, I get it, videos and catch-up TV on the computer?'

'No. I dinnae have a computer, either.'

West flopped back in her chair and huffed in astonishment.

'This is the 21st century, Max, what on earth do you do in the evening?'

'Have you not heard of a thing called the radio? I listen to that. And I read.'

'You read? And what are reading right now?' said West sarcastically. 'No, don't tell me, *Wuthering Heights*?'

'*Meditations*,' said Max, 'Marcus Aurelius.'

'Oh.'

Munro glanced at West and allowed himself a wry grin.

'You know something, Max,' he said, 'you may find this hard to believe but you and I actually have an awful lot in common. However, burgeoning friendships aside, it doesnae detract from the fact that you've walked two girls home on two consecutive nights and, I'm sorry to say, both are now dead.'

'What? Are you joking me?' said Max, his voice trembling with disbelief. 'You mean Mary? That Mary from the bookies, she's dead too?'

'I'm afraid so.'

'I cannae believe it, I mean… oh, just a wee moment here, you dinnae think I…?'

'For some strange reason, Max,' said Munro with a sigh, 'no, I do not, but it's a strange coincidence, wouldn't you say?'

'Aye, now you mention it. Do you think someone's trying to set me up? That Al Pacino fella, maybe?'

'No, that's highly unlikely, but…'

'Listen, it wasnae me, I'm innocent here. Like I said, I went to the Chinese and…'

'I know, laddie, I know,' said Munro, 'nonetheless, we still need to check your alibi.'

'Aye, fair enough, feel free.'

'Now, can we give you a lift home?'

'What? Is that it? I'm free to go?'

'You're free to go,' said Munro. 'I'll get you an unmarked car, don't want the neighbours talking now, do we?'

* * *

West pulled on her coat and stood scowling by the door, impatiently tapping her foot as Munro, lost in a world of his own, sat casually scrolling through his phone.

'Are we going or what?' she said. 'Not only am I losing weight as we speak but I'm dehydrating at an alarming rate too.'

'Och, sorry Charlie,' said Munro, 'I have to make a couple of calls, do you think you could find the hotel by yourself?'

'Probably not,' said West, zipping her coat, 'it's dark out and I'm single and female.'

Munro smiled as he dialled.

'Will I get Max to walk you over?'

'I'll see you there.'

* * *

West, despite feeling dead on her feet and in desperate need of a soothing bath, looked radiantly relaxed as she sat alone at the bar, sipping a vodka and orange and contemplating just how much she could order off the menu without throwing up.

'About time,' she said as Munro reached for the glass of malt, 'it's a Glenfarclas, whatever that means.'

'It means it's worth the wait, lassie.'

'Wish I could say the same,' said West, 'what kept you?'

'I had Dougal nip over to the Chinese restaurant with that photo you took to verify Max's alibi.'

'And? Your round.'

'How many have you had?'

'Just the two.'

'It all checks out,' said Munro as he ordered more drinks, 'they even told Dougal what he ordered.'

'Good, what else?'

'Else?' said Munro, draining his glass. 'I'm not sure what you mean.'

'I wasn't born yesterday,' said West, 'come on, spit it out.'

'I had a word with the D.C.I. about Don. He was, to say the least, none too pleased to get the call.'

'I'm not surprised. I bet he was fuming.'

'Aye, he was,' said Munro, 'but not over Don. He's away to Majorca in the morning and he couldnae find his swimming shorts.'

'Maybe not a bad thing, judging by the size of his waistline. So, what about Don?'

'As of now,' said Munro as he cast an eye over the menu, 'Don is taking an absence of leave. A temporary sabbatical if you will. Pending an inquiry, of course.'

'I see,' said West. 'Shame. So, we're a man down?'

'Aye, but to be fair, I dinnae think you'll notice. Now, why don't you get a table and order, I just have to nip to the… you know?'

'Not before time,' said West, 'what're you having?'

'Chilli squid to start followed by the chicken enchilada with salsa and jalapenos.'

'What? Are you kidding me?'

'What do you think? Back in a tick.'

West grabbed a table towards the back of the restaurant and smiled excitedly as the waiter arrived.

'Two rib-eyes, please,' she said, 'well done. A mountain of chips and a couple of glasses of Merlot, large.'

Chapter 12

Unlike the previous evening when, having arrived late, Munro and West were able to enjoy their supper in the relatively tranquil surroundings of a deserted restaurant, breakfast was an altogether different affair with every table occupied by over-enthusiastic tourists discussing their itineraries in a manner far too audible for his liking.

'I cannae take much more of this,' said Munro, 'they're worse than a gaggle of school kids on a glucose diet. Perhaps if you'd woken at the usual time we'd have missed this kerfuffle.'

'Are you mad?' said West, trying her best to devour her breakfast as fast as possible, 'we're a stone's throw from the office, why would I have got up two hours ago?'

'For the sake of my sanity. If you're not quick, I'll be asking for a doggy bag.'

'Calm down,' said West, 'it's bad enough having to wear the same clothes two days running let alone give myself a dose of indigestion.'

'Surely you've bathed, have you not?'

'Bloody cheek, of course I have.'

'Well then, what's the problem? Come on Charlie, or I'll be helping myself to that black pudding. Chop chop.'

Dougal, as usual, was already at his desk checking the weekend weather forecast on one laptop whilst downloading the film from the beach on another.

'Morning,' he said as Munro and West entered the office, 'how was the hotel? Can I get you a tea?'

'Thanks, Dougal,' said Munro, 'the hotel was satisfactory to say the least. Mattress was a wee bit soft for my liking but you cannae have everything.'

'Good. There's no sign of D.S. Cameron yet, sir. Will I give him a call?'

Munro cast a sideways glance at West, pulled off his coat and sat down.

'Something you need to know, Dougal,' he said, 'and I hope you'll not be too upset, after all, you and Don have worked together for quite a while now, I imagine.'

'What is it? Has something happened?'

'In a manner of speaking,' said Munro, 'let's just say Don no longer has a future in public relations.'

'Sorry?'

'It seems he was a wee bit heavy-handed when he collected Max from the estate agent's office yesterday. Rather than ask if he'd like to help us further with our inquiry, he opted to introduce his face to the desk instead. Naturally, when something as soft as a cheek meets something as hard as a desk, some damage will occur. As a result, Don is on… temporary leave.'

'I see,' said Dougal as he poured the tea. 'Oh well, just the three of us, then?'

'You're not upset?' said West.

'No. It had to happen sooner or later, miss. I could see it coming.'

'Well, that's the mourning period over with then.'

'So, Dougal,' said Munro, 'once you've had your tea, I need you to pop over to the estate agent's office and get a couple of statements.'

'Nae bother, sir. Who am I looking for?'

'Lizzie Paton, she's the receptionist, and Max's boss, a Mr. Mulrennan.'

'Okey dokey, before I go, these are for you.'

Dougal grabbed the print-outs from his desk, neatly stapled in the top left-hand corner and passed them out.

'DVLA,' he said, 'a list of all the registered Astras in the area, all the black ones, that is. I've separated the info out to make it easier to read: registration numbers on pages one and two, owners' details pages three to seven.'

'Most efficient,' said Munro.

'I've also got that film from the camera on the beach, I'll take a look when I get back. Oh, and something else, we had a call this morning from the bookshop on the High Street, said they've a book for D.S. Cameron, he ordered it a week or two ago.'

'Well, you best let him know,' said Munro, 'I can see no harm in that. Although I must say, Don doesnae strike me as the literary kind.'

'Probably something to do with cage-fighting,' said West.

'No, no,' said Dougal, smiling as he pulled on his coat, 'it's called "Investigative Psychology", it's about criminal profiling, that kind of thing.'

* * *

West, feeling lethargic after a more than substantial breakfast, flicked disinterestedly through the information sheets before tossing them to one side and sighing as she stared into space.

'It's like one of those MENSA tests,' she said, mumbling to herself as she cradled her cup of tea, 'write the next number in the sequence or spot the odd one out.'

'What's that?' said Munro, distracted by the repetitive ping from one of Dougal's computers.

'This list. I mean, really, where's it going to get us?'

'Sorry, Charlie,' said Munro, 'would you just see what that infernal racket is about, I cannae hear myself think.'

West ambled begrudgingly across the office and checked the laptop.

'Emails,' she said, 'from the lab by the looks of it. I'll turn the volume down.'

'Thank you. So, what were you saying?'

'Oh nothing, just griping about these bloody Astras.'

'What of them?'

'Well,' said West, returning to her seat, 'what can we possibly ascertain from wasting a day or two, or three even, by driving all over town just to look at them? It's like searching for a needle in a haystack when we don't even know if there's a needle. Or, for that matter, what it looks like.'

'Right enough,' said Munro, 'but that needle could be something which belonged to Agnes or Mary, so even if there's just the smallest possibility that a needle may exist, we have to look for it.'

'Yeah, yeah. Suppose you're right.'

* * *

Munro eased himself into Dougal's chair and, rubbing his hands together in anticipation of handling the hardware, surveyed the computers in front of him. According to the laptop on his left, the outlook for the weekend was bright and clear with a brisk wind accompanied by a noticeable drop in temperature. The laptop on the right showed half a dozen unopened emails. Though no stranger to technology, Munro, hand poised tentatively above the mouse, still felt as anxious as a bomb disposal officer deliberating over which wire to cut when it came to deciding whether to click left or right.

'Charlie,' he said, 'I need you here a moment.'

'Mmm?'

'Charlie, my nerves are frazzled.'

'Lovely.'

'Are you listening to me?'

West glanced up looking slightly perplexed.

'Sorry,' she said, 'having a beta-blocker moment. What is it?'

'I need you to open two of these emails for me, lest I cause this thing to self-destruct.'

West, chuckling to herself in the knowledge that, had he really wanted to, he could have opened the emails himself, wandered over and squatted by the desk.

'Right,' she said, 'here we go, first one's from the lab. The bottle we took from Mary's pocket contained approximately 3.5ml of fluid, the dregs basically. Analysis shows liquid constitutes vodka and... blimey, a 68% concentration of ketamine hydrochloride...'

Munro stood and sauntered casually around the room as he listened.

'...no discernible fingerprints but the DNA lifted from the mouth of the bottle matches Mary's.'

'Okay, stop there,' said Munro. 'She had company. She went to the beach with a female friend. How come the lassie she was with didnae drink it? In fact, nobody else drank it or we'd have another body.'

'Unless she mixed it herself. Maybe she had suicidal tendencies.'

'If she did, Charlie, she'd have jumped in the sea. Would've been a damned site easier. No, no. It was either forced down her neck or...'

'Or...' said West, 'maybe the other person had a different drink?'

'Aye. I think that's probably the most likely explanation at this stage,' said Munro, 'one thing's for sure, we now have a double murderer on our hands. Let's just hope he's no aspirations to progress up the ladder to serial. Okay, go on.'

'Right. Oh, interesting. Fingernails. She had fibres under her nails: wool, black, but they don't match anything she was wearing.'

'Both hands?'

'Yup.'

'Chances are she had a wee tussle then, maybe when the ketamine kicked in. Could be anything, a coat or a scarf or a hat, perhaps. Anything else?'

'Nope, that's it. Next one's from pathology, let's cut to the chase... cause of death: respiratory failure commensurate with an O.D.'

'Really?' said Munro, 'not the wound to her neck?'

'Nope. Seems the ketamine overdose did its job before her throat was cut. They reckon with that amount of K in her system her airways were already clogged. She was probably comatose, too.'

'I see, but obviously the killer didn't know that, so he had to make sure that she hadnae simply passed out.'

'Guess so,' said West, 'seems the trauma to the neck was caused by a single incision, left to right, severing the larynx. Approximately 50mm deep.'

'50mm? That's two inches in old money,' said Munro. 'So definitely not the same blade as used on Agnes.'

'No, bigger but relatively thin. Something like a filleting knife or a...'

Munro, concerned by the unexpected pause, turned to see West gazing at the screen, her chin resting on the desk and her eyes blinking rapidly.

'What is it, Charlie?' he said softly.

'Bloods,' said West, clearing her throat, a slight tremble to her voice. 'When they were testing for toxins they found abnormally high levels of progesterone and oestrogen. Mary Campbell was pregnant.'

'Och, dear God, no. The poor... how far was she... I mean, would she have known?'

'Nine weeks,' said West as she went back to her desk, buried her head in her hands and stared glumly at the sheet of meaningless numbers.

* * *

Munro stood by the window and gazed pensively out across the supermarket car park, the sun glinting off the discarded trolleys and shards of broken glass.

'I wonder if a vet has cause to use a filleting knife?' he said, rhetorically. 'After all, he'd be a dab hand with a blade and he'd have access to a wide selection too. Not to mention the ketamine. Let's see if Mary Campbell knew a vet, perhaps there's a connection there. Charlie, I said…'

West slammed her pen on the desk and threw her head back, groaning in frustration.

'It's no good,' she said, rubbing her eyes, 'I can't take it, this is winding me up.'

'What is?' said Munro, as he scribbled "vet" on a notepad and stuck it to Dougal's computer, 'is it Mary Campbell?'

'No. I don't know. It's these bloody registration numbers, they're doing my head in. I just can't concentrate.'

'An inability to concentrate is often brought about by a sub-conscious desire to focus on something else.'

'Is that a fact?'

'Aye. It is,' said Munro. 'Get it off your chest and you'll see I'm right.'

'What if there isn't anything on my chest?' said West.

'I'm listening.'

'Okay. Okay. Max. Despite the fact he's our only suspect, we had to let him go cos we don't have anything on him, right? He just happens to have been in the right place at the wrong time.'

'Correct,' said Munro. 'Not that we're ruling him out, but the man's an alibi for last night too.'

'I know, I know,' said West, tapping the pen on the desk, 'things is, it's not Max that's bugging me. It's somebody else.'

'Go on.'

'If you think I'm going mad, just tell me to shut up and get a grip but there's someone else who just happened to be around soon after, very soon after, both Agnes and Mary were found. Don.'

Munro, interrupted by the muffled strains of the theme to *The Good, the Bad and the Ugly*, held his hand aloft, pulled his phone from his pocket and stared blankly at West as he took the call.

'Dougal,' he said, 'before you overwhelm me with your news, I've a question for you. Agnes Craig.'

'Aye, sir. What about her?'

'I understand you were first on the scene, after uniform found her. Is that correct?'

'Aye. Well, no. Well, yes, technically speaking, I suppose so.'

'Once again please, Dougal,' said Munro, raising his eyebrows, 'and try plain English this time.'

'Sorry. Basically I was there just long enough to introduce myself to the constable on the door when D.S. Cameron arrived. I didnae even get to see the body.'

'Is that so? And how was he? D.S. Cameron?'

'Flustered,' said Dougal, 'like he couldnae wait to get inside. Pushed past me, nearly sent me flying down the stairs. Told me to wait outside.'

'Okay, thanks, Dougal,' said Munro, 'that's all. Now, what can I do for you?'

'Nothing serious, just to say I'll be a wee while yet but thought you'd like to know Max didnae show for work this morning. Miss Paton's tried calling his mobile a few times but there's no answer.'

'What about his landline?'

'Doesnae have one.'

'Good grief,' said Munro, 'the man's a Luddite after all. Okay Dougal, not to worry, I'll wander over. Be as quick as you can, please.'

'Charlie, I need to check on Max,' said Munro as he terminated the call and reached for his coat, 'he's not arrived for work. I just hope he's not up to anything stupid.'

'Okay,' said West, 'but before you go, you haven't said… I mean, about Don. Will you think about it at least?'

'Oh, I have been, Charlie. I've been thinking about it for a couple days now. And it's troubling me. It's troubling me a great deal.'

Chapter 13

Main Street, not much more than a ten-minute stroll from the police office, was unusually quiet, due in part to a cortege of funeral cars arriving for a service at the Newton Wallacetown Church, three doors down from Max's flat. Munro bowed his head and crossed himself as they filed past, thought of Agnes and, with no surviving relatives to look after her, made a mental note to take care of the funeral arrangements himself.

The entrance to the flat, a single door from the street sandwiched between a mini-mart and the offices of a local charity, seemed deliberately anonymous – no door number, no bell, no letterbox and no knocker. Munro, cringing at the sight of the scuffed, peeling paintwork, hesitated before thumping it with the side of his fist. He stepped back to the kerb just as a window on the upper floor was opening. Max, his head shrouded in what was once a white net curtain, leaned out and smiled.

'Mr. Munro,' he said, 'here, catch.'

Munro caught the keys in one hand, opened the door and, wishing he'd packed a Tyvek suit, paused at the squalid state of the steep, narrow stairwell. The wallpaper, in two minds about staying where it was, leaned away from the cobwebs and drooped lazily towards the floor. The carpet, embellished with a barely discernible pattern and a mixture of stains, most of which appeared to be the colour of curry sauce, was threadbare and worn, whilst the light switch, lacking the screws to hold it in place, dangled precariously from a hole in the wall. He made his way upstairs hoping, without a light to guide him, he wouldn't step on anything soft, sticky or wet.

'Max,' he said, relieved to have reached the summit unscathed, 'I hope I'm not intruding, it's just that folk were worried when you didnae show for work this morning.'

'You mean Lizzie?'

'Aye, in a word.'

'It's okay, Mr. Munro,' said Max, 'my battery was charging. I spoke to her not two minutes ago. She's coming round this evening.'

'Is that so? You must be looking forward to that.'

'Right enough. We'd arranged to go for a bevvy on Friday but after what happened, we just kind of, brought it forward.'

'You sound excited.'

'Aye, I suppose I am. It's sort of like a first date, really. I like Lizzie. I find it easy to talk to her. I feel "comfortable".'

'That's the most important thing, Max,' said Munro with a smile. 'If you can sit in a room with somebody else and not feel compelled to haver, then you're on to a winner.'

'Thanks. As you can see, I've some clearing up to do before she gets here.'

'You're not wrong there. Is that why you didnae go to work?'

'No, no,' said Max, 'I figured with a face like this if I had to show anyone round a house or two, I'd more chance of scaring them off than getting them to make an offer. Can I get you something? Cup of tea, maybe?'

'Aye,' said Munro, glancing around the kitchen – the overflowing dustbin, the crockery piled high in a sink full of murky dish water and empty food wrappers strewn across the counter. 'On second thoughts, you're alright. I've just had some. Are you okay for things? Bin bags? Bleach? Disinfectant? That kind of thing?'

'Aye, thanks, but I'm not an invalid. I can pop out if I need to.'

'Right you are,' said Munro, looking for somewhere to sit, then thinking the better of it, 'so, what will you do with yourself all day? Once you've fumigated this place, that is.'

'Oh, library I expect. Or the bookshop. Why? Am I under house arrest?'

Munro winced as he sneaked a look past the bedroom door.

'No, of course not,' he said, 'but bearing in mind your current circumstances, it's best we know where you are.'

'Very reassuring, Mr. Munro,' said Max as he swept the debris from the counter to the floor, 'I appreciate it.'

'Good. One last thing before I go. Have you thought any more about pressing charges? I'll back you all the way if you decide to go ahead, of course. You have my word on it.'

Max stared in bewilderment at the sink and then the draining board piled high with the remnants of a Chinese takeaway, confused about which to clear first.

'I'm not sure,' he said, frustrated with his indecisiveness, 'I'm just not sure.'

* * *

West, rarely prone to awarding herself a pat on the back, smiled smugly as she cleaned the wipe-board and listened intently to an animated Dougal recount details of the interviews he'd conducted at the estate agent's office.

'I just find it odd, miss,' he said, 'that someone you know and obviously like, I mean, she's carrying a torch for him, it's that obvious, gets belted round the head at your place of work and yet she's reticent to talk about it.'

'Maybe she's embarrassed, Dougal. About showing her feelings. Doesn't want word getting round the office that she and Max might be…'

'No, no, there's something else here, trust me. If she felt like that, then there's no way she'd have kicked off in the first place.'

'Kicked off?'

'Aye,' said Dougal. 'See here, her boss, okay, he says she was completely out of character, as soon as D.S. Cameron walked in the door she went mental, almost as though she recognised him.'

'Doubt it, Dougal. Why does he think that?'

'Just stuff she said, swearing mainly and screaming stuff like "stay away from me".'

'She was probably scared, Dougal,' said West, 'probably thought she was going to get clouted next. I think you're reading too much into it.'

* * *

Upon returning to the office Munro had half expected to see West banging her head against the wall and screaming with frustration as she grappled with the list of Astras. At the very least, he wouldn't have been surprised to find Dougal casually watching two full-length feature films simultaneously on his laptops. What he most certainly did not expect, was to be confronted by the pair of them grinning at him like a couple of Cheshire cats.

'Either you've arranged a surprise party for me,' he said, removing his coat and walking warily to his desk, 'or you've both done something terribly, terribly wrong.'

'You first,' said West.

Dougal pulled the sticky note from his computer and waved it at Munro.

'Bit too cryptic for me, sir,' he said.

'Check all the vets in the area for break-ins,' said Munro as he eyed West suspiciously, 'and see if any of them knew Mary Campbell. There's an outside chance she may have been stepping out with one of them. A vet, I mean.'

'Nae bother. Now, do you want the good news or the bad news?'

'What's the difference?'

'None,' said Dougal, 'just depends how you look at it.'

Munro allowed himself a wry smirk and sat down.

'Go on,' he said.

'I've downloaded the footage from the car park and bingo! Same Astra. Arrives at 8:42pm. Leaves at 11:04pm.'

'Well surely there must be some coverage of the driver, is there not? Getting out of the vehicle? Walking back?'

''Fraid not,' said Dougal. 'I reckon they knew about the camera. They drove way down the back of the car park, completely out of sight, then must've walked the long way round. All we've got is the car arriving and leaving.'

'I'm not entirely sure if that's at all useful,' said Munro, turning his attention to a grinning West. 'Charlie, what are you looking so happy about?'

West picked up the marker and began drawing on the wipe board.

'This,' she said, 'is the registration number of the Astra: EU55 EAS.'

'Indeed it is,' said Munro, 'nothing wrong with your memory, then.'

'Right. Now look. What if the 'E' isn't an 'E'?' said West as she erased the top and middle horizontals. 'What if it's an 'L'? And what if the 'U' is a 'J'? And what if the second 'E' is really an 'F'?'

'We get LJ55 FAS,' said Dougal, flicking through the sheets, 'and it's on the list! Genius, miss. Pure bloody genius.'

'And easily done,' said West, 'just some black tape stuck on the plates and no-one's the wiser.'

'Well done, Charlie,' said Munro, smiling proudly, 'I think you may have a future in the force after all. Dougal, do we…'

'Aye, sir. It's a Mr. Cameron, Drumcoyle Drive, Coylton. It's about four miles away.'

'Good. Charlie, you come with me…'

'Sir!' said Dougal. 'Hold on. Drumcoyle Drive. That's where… I mean, that's D.S. Cameron's address.'

Munro slumped in his seat as if he'd taken a bullet to the chest.

'Oh dear,' he said, wiping his brow, 'oh dear, dear, dear.'

'What'll we do?' said Dougal. 'I mean, everything's pointing to him being…'

'Let me think!' said Munro, irritated by the persistent ring of his phone. 'Okay, look, the first thing we have to do is put Charlie's theory to the test. We need to get a look at that car and it's not going to be easy with Don sitting at home seven days a week.'

Munro clasped his hands beneath his chin and stared at the ceiling.

'Okay,' he said eventually, 'I'm putting my neck on the line here, let's hope it pays off. In the meantime, not a word to anybody about this. Got that?'

'Aye, sir,' said Dougal, 'but what is it you're going to do exactly?'

'You'll find out soon enough, Dougal. You'll find out soon…'

West, annoyed at Munro's reluctance to answer his phone, scowled at him like a schoolmistress about to chastise a pupil.

'Are you going to get that or what?' she said, as it continued to ring. 'It might be important.'

Munro frowned at the screen.

'Well, it's not a number I recognise,' he said angrily, 'so it's either the Bad or the Ugly.'

The stunned expression on Munro's face and the fact that he said nothing at all, made the ensuing silence heavy to bear. His eyes darted between Dougal and West as he hung up.

'I've got a horrible feeling that wasn't the Ugly,' said West.

'Dougal, time for a quiz,' said Munro. 'What do you suppose is the murder capital of the world?'

'Easy. Caracas, Venezuela.'

'Not any more. We've another body.'

'Are you joking me?' said Dougal. 'This is unheard of. Three bodies in three days?'

'Where?' said West.

'A bookshop on the High Street.'

'Waterstone's?' said Dougal. 'That's where D.S. Cameron was headed, to collect that book.'

'Aye,' said Munro as he frantically dialled a number on his phone, 'and so was… Max? D.I. Munro here. Are you still at home? Good. And you've not been out? Okay, listen, I need you to stay exactly where you are. Do not leave the house. D.C. McCrae is on his way over to you now. No, nothing to worry about but it's best if he sits with you a wee while, is that okay? Good. He'll even give you a hand.'

'A hand with what?' said Dougal as he pulled on his coat.

'He'll tell you when you get there,' said Munro, with a crafty grin, 'but I'd take some gloves if I were you. Half a dozen pairs at least. Charlie, you and me, let's go.'

* * *

The crowd outside the bookshop was the largest ever to grace Waterstone's, even for a book-signing by an author of some repute. A paramedic's motorbike and an ambulance blocked the pavement as two uniformed constables, the strain showing on their faces, grew tired of telling the voyeuristic mob to keep back. Munro parked opposite and sat surveying the scene.

'What do we know so far?' said West.

'Not much, Charlie. Female, late thirties. Manageress apparently. Name of Jean Armour. Unless she's a breath in her body, she'll still be in the ladies' toilet by the café.'

'Do we know what happened? I mean, I take it she didn't just have a heart problem?'

'Well, if she didn't, she has now. Come on, let's…'

'Wait, wait, wait,' said West, almost whispering as she tugged at Munro's sleeve, 'over there, look, back of the crowd by the bike.'

'Now, that,' said Munro with a smile, 'is what you call serendipity. Aye, that's the word. Serendipity.'

* * *

'Don. You've a habit of turning up like a bad penny,' said Munro as he took him by the elbow and gently eased him away from the crowd.

'Chief, I didnae expect to see you here.'

'No. I don't suppose you didn't. So, you just happened to be passing, is that it?'

'No, no, I came to collect a book but I cannae get through the door, what's going on?'

'You mean you don't know? You surprise me, Don. The warranty on your sixth sense must have expired. It's just another fatality, just another…'

'Of course, had to be. I should've guessed, I mean, with this many folk…'

Cameron paused as he noticed West, flanked by two uniformed police officers, approach from across the street.

'Don,' said Munro, 'can you complete this well-known saying: You do not have to say anything. But…?'

'…it may harm your defence if you do not mention when questioned something you later rely on in court.'

'Good, that's that out the way. Now, as a wee treat, Charlie here has arranged a lift for you. These two gentlemen have a car waiting.'

'A lift? What do you mean, a…?'

'Donald Cameron. I'm arresting you on suspicion of the murders of Agnes Craig and Mary Campbell. Oh, and whoever's in there, but you probably know who she is already.'

* * *

Apart from a spattering of what appeared to be ketchup tainting one wall, the toilet cubicle, with its polished white tiles, shiny chrome tissue dispenser and spotless sanitary bin was, much to Munro's delight, as clean as the bookstore's café. The lifeless body of Jean Armour lay slumped to one side, her head uncomfortably wedged against the wall. Were it not for the obvious stab wound to the neck and another beneath her blood-stained blouse she looked, with her eyes closed and mouth shut, not unlike somebody who'd simply passed out from an excess of alcohol.

'He's getting sloppy,' said Munro, 'this wasnae planned like the other two, it was rushed, impulsive. The question is, why?'

'Maybe he knew we were on his tail,' said West.

'Oh aye, and he just wanted to squeeze another one in before he got caught? No. Look, he was meticulous about the attacks on Agnes and Mary. He was patient enough to wait until they were alone. He went to the trouble of drugging them before killing them. Both young, both single, both murdered in the dead of night in their own homes. Now we have Miss Armour here – hacked to death in broad daylight in a public space. It doesnae make any sense.'

'So…' said West, 'what if he's getting scared, upping the ante and attacking women at random?'

'No. He's too methodical for that.'

'And that's why you're not convinced about Don. Are you?'

'I'll need some persuading,' said Munro, 'but at least if he's in our custody for the next 24 hours it gives us a chance to have a look at his car and, if no other bodies turn up while we've got him, well then I'm happy to be proved wrong.'

'And if another does?'

'Then,' said Munro with a sigh, 'you'd best be prepared for the kind of press conference that'll make you wish you worked in a supermarket.'

West looked at Munro, his tortured expression suggesting he was in urgent need of root canal surgery.

'There's something else, isn't there?' she said. 'What is it?'

'The link, Charlie,' said Munro, biting his bottom lip. 'Miss Armour here doesnae fit the mould. What on earth connects her to the other two?'

'Well,' said West, flummoxed, 'perhaps there's…'

'Charlie, it's not the kind of question you can answer off the cuff in a toilet cubicle. Think about it later. Right now, observations please.'

West leaned forward and scrutinised the body, from the upturned hands hanging limply by its side to the almost relaxed posture and completely inconsonant look of peace on her face.

'She didn't die instantly,' said West, 'she slipped away, slowly. Single stab wound to the front of the neck, my guess is that was to render her speechless, like Mary. Lots of blood from the chest wound, though. Her blouse is soaked. Looks like he scored a bullseye there. Probably bled to death.'

'Good. What else?'

West stared blankly at the body, turned to Munro and shrugged her shoulders.

'There isn't much else,' she said.

'Come on, Charlie,' said Munro, 'you can do better than that, concentrate on the circumstances, not the body. Okay, look, whoever did this was behind her when she came in, I mean, right behind her. If she was here to answer a call of nature, she didnae get the chance. The seat lid's down and her underwear is still around her waist. She didnae even come close to locking the door.'

'Point taken,' said West, 'so…?'

'What do you think? We need to find out who followed her in, of course.'

'Where would we be without CCTV, eh?'

'A damned sight better off,' said Munro, 'there was a time when a camera was used to capture a special moment in your life, a keepsake to look back on, not used to track you 24 hours a day or take an impromptu photo of your backside.'

* * *

Miss Clow considered herself to be a natural born leader with a flair for delegating and enough experience in the retail world to rapidly rise above what she considered to be the demeaning rank of assistant manager. Those who worked with her, however, saw only an arrogant authoritarian with a lust for power and a complete lack of humility. Riled by the fact that she was not an integral part of the investigation, she begrudgingly led Munro and West upstairs to the office, her stern expression made all the worse thanks to the severity of her hairstyle – scraped back and knotted in the tightest of buns on the back of her head.

'Tell me, Miss Clow,' said Munro as she claimed the only chair available and settled in front of a bank of six small monitors, 'were you friends with Miss Armour?'

'I was not. We didn't socialise and we rarely worked the same shifts.'

'I see. So, you cannae tell us anything about her personal life then?'

'No. I cannot. Look, I don't mean to sound callous, Inspector, but I hardly knew the woman. I'm only here because the police insisted. It's my day off. I'm supposed to be relaxing.'

'I quite understand,' said Munro, 'death can be so… inconvenient.'

'Well?' said Clow tersely, 'I haven't got all day. What is it you need to see, exactly?'

'I want you find the moment Miss Armour heads for the toilets.'

Clow turned her attention to the monitor second from left, a camera situated above the café area, rewound the film until Armour came into view and hit "play". Munro and West watched intently for what seemed like an eternity.

'That's almost three minutes,' said West, 'too long. And no-one's followed.'

'Okay,' said Munro, 'there's another possibility. Perhaps our man didnae follow her after all. Perhaps he was waiting for her. Rewind please, Miss Clow, go back about half an hour and play it again.'

Clow checked her watch and sighed.

'Half an hour? I don't have the time to…'

'You can fast forward,' said Munro sternly, 'and slow down as soon as you see anyone in desperate need of the facilities.'

West looked nervously at the clock in the corner of the screen and winced as the minutes flew by.

'That's two women in and two women out,' she said, 'not exactly teeming with witnesses, is it?'

'It's too early,' said Clow, 'we don't get busy until lunchtime and as for those two, I can almost guarantee they've popped in off the street. Some folk seem to think we're nothing more than a public convenience.'

'Stop!' said West. 'There, someone in a black coat and a hoodie and he looks like he's bursting. And here comes Armour. What do you think?'

'Well,' said Munro, 'he's of a similar height and build to you know who, but as we cannae see his face…'

'Do you think he'd have time though?' said West, 'I mean, to come in here, nip home and change, and come back again?'

'Oh, aye, he's only four miles away, he'd do it easy. He could even change in the back of his car. Okay, Miss Clow, you can resume playback now.'

Exactly six minutes and forty-eight seconds later, the hooded figure returned and, with his head down and hands buried deep in his pockets, turned in the opposite direction and scurried from view towards the back of the store.

'Wait, wait, wait!' said an infuriated West. 'Where's he going? Why's he going the wrong way? For Christ's sake, what's down there?'

'Nothing,' said Clow, 'it leads to the loading bay outside.'

'Oh, great. Any cameras down there?'

'I'm not head of security, Sergeant, but I dare say there'll be one by the gates on Arthur Street.'

'Miss Clow,' said Munro, handing her a business card, 'if it's not too much trouble, what with your busy schedule and all, would you send the footage from all those cameras to D.C. McCrae at this email address, please? We'll need it as soon as possible.'

'I'll do my best, Inspector, but I can't guarantee it will be today.'

'Oh, but it will, Miss Clow,' said Munro bluntly. 'It will be today. Now, one more thing before we go. I assume Miss Armour would have arrived for work wearing a coat and no doubt carrying a bag. Where would she keep them?'

'That's her coat,' said Clow, feeling unjustifiably berated as she pointed to the back of the door, 'the dark blue one on the hanger. And she normally keeps her bag in that drawer, just there.'

West patted down the coat and, finding the pockets empty, draped it over her arm and waited while Munro snapped on a pair of gloves and pulled the bag from the drawer.

'Forgive me for asking, Miss Clow,' he said as they made their way out, 'but would I be right in thinking you're of a vegetarian persuasion?'

'I most certainly am. What of it?'

'Have you ever been to the Holy Isle?'

'I have not.'

'You should go. I hear they do a cracking humble pie.'

* * *

Munro, arms outstretched against the steering wheel, watched despairingly as the crowd outside the bookstore lingered in the morbid hope of catching a glimpse of the body as it was ferried to the ambulance while West, ever curious to know why women were so fond of handbags, rummaged through Armour's belongings and found nothing that couldn't be carried in the pockets of a jacket: a lipstick and a mascara; house keys; twenty-seven pence in loose change; a small purse containing one five and one ten pound note, an assortment of bank cards and a receipt from Marks and Spencer; and her phone.

'She either wasn't very popular or enjoyed her own company too much,' she said as she scrolled through the short list of contacts. 'There's no record of any texts she might have sent and the last one she received was more than three weeks ago, and that was from her service provider. No incoming calls since whenever and uh-oh, get this, she rang somebody yesterday. No name though, just a number.'

'She rang an unidentified number yesterday,' said Munro, intrigued, 'and today she's dead? May I?'

Munro took the phone, studied the number and, glancing at West, dialled. The call went to voicemail. He hung up and dialled again.

'Jeannie,' came the reply, 'look, I've told you before, there's no point in you calling me. I have a heap of stuff to do just now, look, I'm sorry but...'

'Max.'

The pause was brief.

'Who is this?'

'Max, it's D.I. Munro. I think you've some explaining to do. Stay put.'

Munro passed the phone to West and fastened his seat belt.

'Hold on,' she said, 'before we go, you know lots of stuff about everything, I need to ask you something.'

'Okay, but be brief, Charlie, we don't have time to…'

'Which do you think is better, the Mediterranean diet or the Atkins diet?'

'What?' said Munro. 'Have you…? Any kind of diet is an exercise in futility, lassie, why on earth do you ask?'

'Because I've been on a starvation diet since seven o'clock this morning and if we don't eat something soon, by which I mean now, there's a very good chance I may resort to cannibalism.'

Chapter 14

Dougal, wearing a look of utter disgust, carefully removed his coat and, holding it carefully betwixt his thumbs and forefingers, hung it over the back of his chair.

'I'm not being funny, sir,' he said, 'but I need a shower. There's all manner of wildlife crawling round that flat.'

'You should be proud of yourself, Dougal,' said Munro, as he placed a carrier bag of food on the table, 'I'm sure Max is incredibly grateful. It's nice to help folk out, you know, those a little less fortunate than yourself.'

'Aye, right enough. Crossing the street, maybe, not sterilising a contaminated area. The place was a health hazard.'

'Well you've done us all proud,' said West, plucking a bacon sandwich from the bag, 'and because of you, Max can now have a romantic evening at home.'

'Oh please, miss,' said Dougal, 'I think I may heave if you say anymore. So, is that him in the clear then, sir?'

'Aye,' said Munro, 'well, not exactly. Let's just say he's not the focus of our inquiry for now. I feel sorry for the lad. Seems Miss Armour, may she rest in peace, had the hots for him. Poor fellow couldnae cope with all the attention.'

'So what now?'

'Check your email,' said Munro, opening the carrier bag, 'Charlie, there were four sandwiches in here, now there are two.'

'That's right,' said West, 'one for you and one for Dougal.'

'Good grief, lassie, you're worse than a feral dog with a dose of the worms. As I was saying, Dougal, check your email, you should have the video from the bookstore. Chap in a black coat and a hoodie, the usual, please. Then see if you cannae find a link between Agnes, Mary Campbell and Miss Armour, there must be something that connects them, a shared interest. Something. Anything. We're away just now to have a wee chat with D.S. Cameron.'

'Up to his house?' said Dougal. 'Is that not a wee bit risky?'

'Och, he's not home, Dougal, he's downstairs. Would you believe, he's kindly offered to help us with the inquiry. Generous of him, wouldn't you say?'

* * *

It wasn't being interned on the wrong side of the bars that bothered Cameron. He was strong enough, old enough and hard enough to deal with the inconvenience of having to prove his innocence from the accused's side of the desk. It was the sneaky sideways glances and snide comments from colleagues he'd once considered friends that he found difficult to cope with. He sat doubled over with his hands hanging between his legs like a boxer who knew he'd lost the bout on points, failing to stir even when Munro and West entered the interview room and took a seat opposite him.

'Don,' said Munro with a hefty sigh, 'I'm not happy about this, I'm not happy at all but something's come to light and we've a few questions that need answering.'

Cameron, looking downcast and beaten, slowly turned his head and stared vacuously at West. A half smile crossed his weathered face.

'You think I did it?' he said. 'You think I killed those three girls?'

West hesitated, surprised at how much he seemed to have aged beneath the harsh overhead light.

'How do you know the third is dead?' she said.

'Very good,' said Cameron, laughing, 'you've got me. Well, you'd best switch the tape on, then we can get this over with.'

'No, no,' said Munro. 'I'm not recording this. I just want your help. Okay?'

Cameron sat up and folded his arms.

'Okay,' he said, 'shoot.'

'Your car, Don. What car do you drive?'

'Are you joking me?' said Cameron. 'You know full well what car I drive, you've been in it. It's a Golf. Grey, five door, in case you've forgotten.'

'And what about the Vauxhall?' said Munro. 'Astra, black, five door, likewise.'

'Astra? I dinnae have… oh hold on, that clapped-out thing? How do you know about the Astra?'

'So you admit to owning it?' said West.

'Aye, but it's not been used in years, it's ancient. It's not even taxed.'

'And where is it now?'

'In the garage of course,' said Cameron, 'but why…?'

'Keys please, Don,' said Munro, holding out his hand, 'we need to take a look.'

'Are you serious?'

'We could a get a warrant, if you'd prefer.'

Cameron pulled a bunch of keys from his jacket pocket and slid them across the desk.

'These'll get you in the house,' he said, 'car key's in the kitchen, on a hook by the back door.'

* * *

Drumcoyle Drive, with its modern semi-detached houses replete with manicured front lawns, was a quiet residential street well-suited to aspiring middle class families with two-point-four children and a burning desire to park a Lexus on the drive. For an ageing detective with an eye for aesthetics, however, the bland uniformity of the characterless facades was nothing more than an underwhelming example of architectural complacency.

'Definition of suburbia, Charlie?' said Munro as he parked the car.

'A breeding ground for banality?'

Munro smiled.

'I think we need a divorce,' he said, heading for the house, 'you're beginning to sound too much like myself.'

West, astute enough to know that the unexpected arrival of a strange car in a tight-knit neighbourhood might compel the more inquisitive residents to reach for the lawnmower in an attempt to surreptitiously snoop on the visitors, paused by the door and glanced up and down the deserted street before joining Munro inside.

'Would you look at this,' he said, waving an arm at the crammed bookshelves in the lounge, 'it's all art and literature: Gaugin, Monet, Pissarro, Hardy, Burns, Wordsworth…'

'Probably nothing to do with Don,' said West cynically, as she made for the kitchen, 'I doubt he's made it past Winnie the Pooh.'

'What does his wife do exactly?'

'No idea, we can ask Dougal,' said West, waving the car key, 'come on, I'm dying to take a look.'

* * *

West, heart pounding, stood to one side and anxiously held her breath as Munro unlocked the garage door and slowly heaved it open, her optimistic enthusiasm fading into thin air as she caught sight of the number plate.

'Crap!' she said, stamping her feet like an eight-year-old throwing a tantrum, 'crap, crap, crap! Oh, well, that's that then. Still, it was only a theory, I suppose. A ridiculously stupid, bloody pathetic, ill-conceived... what are you doing?'

Munro, oblivious to West's self-demeaning rant, stood with his hands clasped habitually behind his back and viewed the car with a degree of consternation – the lack of dust on the wheel rims or cobwebs hanging from the wing mirrors was not symptomatic of a car which had lain idle for any period of time. He stepped forward and placed his right hand, palm down on the bonnet, surprised to find it was not as cold to the touch as he'd expected.

'Charlie,' he said, squatting by the grill, the faint smell of burnt engine oil filling his nostrils as he ran finger over the number plate, 'there's something sticky here, residue of some sort. Adhesive maybe. Nip round the back and take a look at the other one.'

West bounded to the rear of the car with renewed vigour.

'Can't see it,' she said, cursing in frustration, 'it's too tight to the bloody wall.'

Munro pulled on a pair of gloves, opened the driver's door and ducked his head inside.

'Bag please, Charlie,' he said, picking small bobbles of black wool from the back of the seat, 'we need to get these off, no doubt they'll be a perfect match for the fibres found on young Mary Campbell.'

West, her adrenaline levels on the rise, crossed her fingers behind her back as Munro placed the key in the ignition and gave it a flick. The engine, unsurprisingly, started first time. He edged it forward a few feet, enough to get a good look at the rear and nodded approvingly at the sound of West yelping with delight.

'I knew it, I bloody knew it! Am I a genius or what?' she said jokingly.

'You're no Einstein yet, Charlie,' said Munro with a grin, 'but you're getting there. Now, let's see what delights yon boot has to offer.'

West popped it open and punched Munro playfully on the arm as they stared in unison at the black, woollen pea coat and a grey, hooded sweat-top lying crumpled in a heap.

'Shall we call it in?' she said.

'No, no,' said Munro, 'lock it up. We'll have a wee nosey round the house first.'

West scampered to the kitchen as Munro, eyes narrowed and brow creased with the subtlest of frowns, cast a curious eye around the lounge – the black leather three-piece suite strewn with cushions, discarded clothes and magazines; the wall-mounted flat screen TV hanging above the bricked-up fireplace and the collection of dirty mugs and unopened mail scattered across the coffee table – until his attention was drawn inexplicably once more to the shelves where every book bar one, a modest paperback with a burgundy spine, was aligned with the fastidious precision of somebody afflicted with OCD. He raised a finger and gently pushed it back to its rightful place as West returned from the kitchen.

'Look what I've got,' she said, holding up a roll of black insulating tape, 'and there's a knife missing from the block, one of the long ones.'

'Upstairs,' said Munro, 'you take the bathroom.'

* * *

Munro, believing a clean house to have the same therapeutic effect on the state of one's mental health as the unconditional love of a cocker spaniel, grimaced at the slovenly similarity between Cameron's bedroom and that of Mr. Andrew Maxwell Stewart. He flicked on the light and picked his way across the floor – skilfully negotiating the soiled socks, several pairs of boxer shorts and an empty bowl of cereal – towards the bed, only one side of which had been slept in. Lying on the other was an upturned copy of *Spanish for Beginners*. The bedside cabinet, he observed, was cluttered with the usual paraphernalia: a reading lamp, an alarm clock, a half empty tumbler of water, a pair of nail scissors and a small, white plastic bottle of what appeared to be paracetamol. He picked it up, intrigued by the label.

'Oi, Jimbo!' yelled West from the bathroom, 'come see what I've found.'

Munro shook his head and smiled at her blatant familiarity. "Inspector", he relented, was perhaps a little too formal. "Chief" or "Guv" he could live with. But "Jimbo"?

'You deaf or what?' she said, appearing in the doorway.

'Did you know Don was on sleeping pills?' said Munro, 'Zolpidem?'

'That's not all he's on,' said West, holding up two 10ml vials of ketamine HCl, 'and there's a pack of sterile syringes in the cabinet too.'

Munro sat on the bed and bagged the bottle of pills, his shoulders sagging with disappointment.

'Okay,' he said reluctantly, 'call it in, Charlie.'

'What about the rest of the house?'

'I think we've enough to be going on with, don't you? I want the whole house sealed off, dusted and swabbed for any trace of Agnes or Mary, same goes for the car. Tell them to pull it apart if they have to.'

'No probs,' said West. 'So, are we going to charge him?'

'Not yet. Not until forensics give us something to bite on. I'm away to the office, get uniform to drop you back as soon as you can, high time we had another word with Don.'

* * *

Dougal, displaying the dexterity of an octopus in a bed full of oysters, was using both computers to scour the social media and the plethora of pages associated with anyone bearing the same names as the deceased when a fatigued-looking Munro returned and slumped wearily in a chair.

'You look like you need a brew, sir,' he said, reaching for the kettle.

'Aye,' said Munro, 'if you've one that's 40% proof, I'll not say no.'

'That bad?'

'I'm afraid so, Dougal. Charlie was right about the number plates and we found a black coat and a sweat top in the boot of the car.'

'That's a relief, cos I drew a blank with the fella on the video, he just vanished into thin air. So, I take it this means it's not looking good for D.S. Cameron, then?'

'Well,' said Munro, 'bearing in mind we recovered a stash of ketamine from his bathroom, I'd have to say no. It's not looking good at all. To be honest, he's as good as wearing a noose around his neck already.'

'That's too bad,' said Dougal, 'still, he's not swinging yet.'

'Just a matter of time, laddie, just a matter of time. Incidentally Dougal, would you happen to know what D.S. Cameron's wife does for a living?'

'Aye, sir, teacher I believe. Art and design.'

'Is that so?' said Munro. 'Well, that would explain the books then.'

'Sorry?'

'Nothing. Do you know where?'

''Fraid not,' said Dougal, 'cannae be far though, the college maybe? Will I find out?'

'No, no. It's not important. So, progress?'

'I've been looking for the missing link, sir.'

'And?'

'I cannae find it.'

'Now you know how Darwin felt,' said Munro.

'Darwin?'

'It's a joke, Dougal. Take it home, let it evolve.'

'Right. Well, moving on, I'm still digging around but so far, I'm sorry to say, of the twenty-eight Mary

Campbells, seven Agnes Craigs and six Jeanne Armours who use social media, not one of them is ours.'

Munro sat back, cradled his cup of tea and stared silently into space.

'You're awful quiet, sir,' said Dougal, 'are you okay?'

'I've an itch, Dougal, and I cannae reach it.'

'Do you want a ruler?'

'I'll not reach it with a ruler, not unless I crack my head in two.'

'I'm not even going to ask,' said Dougal, smiling as West burst through the door.

'Those bloody stairs,' she said, panting, 'they'll be the death of me. Stick the kettle on please, Dougal, I'm parched.'

'Best make that a takeaway, Dougal,' said Munro, 'come on, Charlie, we've a meeting to go to.'

Chapter 15

Cameron, frustrated with nothing to do but sit and wait in the confines of the interview room with not even a book to read or a window to gaze from, cursed impatiently as he checked his watch for the umpteenth time.

'I hope you've not lost my keys,' he said, sneering as West and Munro entered the room.

'No, no. They're quite safe,' said Munro, 'I'll return them just as soon as we're done.'

'Done?' said Cameron. 'I thought all you wanted to do was take a look at that heap of rust in the garage?'

'Aye, we did. And forensics are giving it the once over as we speak.'

'Forensics?'

Munro leaned back in his seat, folded his arms and glanced at the tape machine.

'Are you going to switch that on?' said Cameron.

'That all depends on you, Don. On how much you're willing to co-operate, after all, you've not been charged with anything. Not yet, anyway.'

'Makes no odds to me, chief, I've nothing to fear. But I'll tell you this, if I'm not out of here soon, I'll make sure the world and his wife know how you've wrongfully arrested a fellow police officer.'

'Och, Don, it's not a wrongful arrest, you know that…' said Munro as he leaned forward and locked Cameron with a penetrating gaze, his ice-blue eyes drilling into his head, 'and a word to the wise – I'm not too keen on threats. I've a habit of taking them rather too… personally.'

Cameron, ruffled by Munro's intimidating tone and the subsequent silence, swallowed hard and turned to face West, his bleary, brown eyes searching for some compassionate respite.

'Cómo estás, Don?' she said, smiling softly, 'va todo bien?'

'Va todo… what?'

'Oh come on, it's pretty basic Spanish. You do speak Spanish, don't you? Hablas español?'

'I was learning,' said Cameron, glancing furtively at Munro, 'I havenae got to grips with it yet.'

'So, you're not fluent?' said West.

'No.'

'Why the interest?'

'I was going to surprise May.'

'May?' said Munro, raising his eyebrows.

'The wife.'

'That's a pretty name,' said Munro, 'just as well she wasnae born in December. Had she a sudden yearning for paella or a few bowls of tapas then?'

Cameron bit his lip.

'If you must know, I'd planned a wee trip,' he said. 'Two weeks, Granada. I was going to impress her with my grasp of the language.'

'And you're not going now?'

'Given the present circumstances, I'd say that was pretty obvious, wouldn't you?'

'So you were teaching yourself, is that it?' said West. 'I mean, that would explain the textbook in your bedroom.'

'You are joking me, right?' said Cameron. 'Have you seen how they spell their words? It's hard enough trying to read it, let alone speak it.'

'So?'

'So I was going to night school, okay? Once a week.'

'And where was that, exactly?' said Munro.

'Troon. Marr College.'

Cameron shifted uneasily in his seat as Munro, drumming his fingers on the desk, stared right through him, a look of perplexity on his face.

'I do apologise,' he said as he stood and headed for the door, 'I shan't be a moment, make yourself at home.'

* * *

Munro strolled to the end of corridor and, forsaking the four flights of steps, pulled his phone from his pocket and called the office.

'Dougal,' he said, his voice hushed, 'Marr College. D.S. Cameron went to night school there – Spanish for beginners. Find out who else was in his class, would you?'

'No hay problema, jefe.'

'Good grief, laddie, if you dinnae stop havering, there'll be a grande problema. Comprendes?'

'Sir. While you're on, something you need to know. We just got a second report through from pathology. It's about Mary Campbell.'

* * *

Cameron, his face riddled with boredom, barely flinched as Munro walked solemnly around the desk and returned to his seat.

'So, Don,' he said, 'let's talk about the Astra.'

'That'll be a riveting conversation.'

'I had no idea that vehicle was such a remarkable feat of engineering. How long did you say since you last used it?'

'I didn't,' said Cameron, 'but it has to be a year, at least. Maybe more.'

'Astounding,' said Munro. 'Aye, that's the word. Astounding. A year off the road and not even a flat battery.'

'Are you serious?'

'Started first time. But what's more intriguing is why someone would want to disguise the number plates.'

'Come again?'

'Wee pieces of tape stuck on the plates to change the letters,' said Munro, 'like an F to an E for example.'

'Och, you're off your head,' said Cameron, 'I told you, no-one's been in that garage for months and I'm the only who'd...'

'And in the boot,' said West, 'we found a black overcoat and a hoodie, both about your size, I reckon. And guess what? They match the outfit worn by whoever killed Jean Armour in the bookshop.'

'No, no, no, you're making this up. You're just trying to get me to...'

Cameron froze as West pulled a clear, plastic bag from her pocket and placed it on the table.

'Do you remember what killed Agnes?' she said. 'And Mary Campbell?'

Cameron's eyes flitted between West and Munro.

'Aye, of course,' he said, clearing his throat, 'they were stabbed, they were both...'

'Ketamine overdose,' said West, 'that's what killed them. And we found these in your bathroom. Not looking good is it, Don?'

'Listen, if you're trying to pin this on me, it won't stick, it...'

'Oh, it will stick,' said Munro, 'it will stick like mud. The ketamine. You've been self-medicating, have you not? Where'd you get it?'

Cameron, staring at the vials on the table, said nothing.

'I know, it must've been the vet's surgery,' said Munro, 'the one that had the break-in, near Craigie.'

'Aye,' said Cameron, 'that'll be it. The vet's. Near Craigie.'

West nearly fell off her seat as Munro stood abruptly and brought his fist crashing down on the desk causing Cameron to recoil.

'Listen up, Don!' he said through gritted teeth. 'I'll have none of your jiggery-pokery here, understand? There was no break-in at the surgery, you got it from the hospital, am I right?'

Cameron smirked at West and raised his eyebrows.

'You should get something for that temper of yours,' he said facetiously, 'or one day you'll explode. Do something you might regret.'

'That day may be closer than you think, Don,' said Munro, menacingly, 'and you'll not want to be on the receiving end, I can assure you, there's a headstone or two'll testify to that. So, the night you were stabbed, you didnae go to A&E, did you? You went to find Doctor Kelly. And he stitched you up.'

'In more ways than one,' said West, smirking, 'he's on his way over now and, ironically, his career's heading for the morgue, too. He gave you the ketamine didn't he? And the sleeping pills.'

Cameron, unwilling to relent, sat back in his chair, combed his fingers through his hair and glowered at Munro.

'You're clutching at straws,' he said defiantly, 'all this… this so-called evidence, it's all circumstantial, it'll never stand-up in…'

'Come, come,' said Munro, 'you should know better than that, Don. Circumstantial it may be, but it's overwhelming nonetheless. Enough for a conviction.'

'You are joking?' said Cameron, laughing nervously. 'Listen, if that's all you've got, you'll have to let me go in approximately…'

'No, no, let's not be hasty, Don. See, I'm feeling in a generous mood, so I'm going to upgrade your package and extend your stay free of charge. Now, where were we? Oh, aye, who stabbed you?'

'Come again?'

'I'm not in the habit of repeating myself,' said Munro sternly.

'I told you, the bampot in the off-licence.'

'Is that so? Big fella was he?'

'Aye, I'd say so,' said Cameron. 'Taller than me, well built.'

'And how did he stab you? Like this?' said Munro, thrusting his arm forward.

'Aye, pretty much, why?'

'Because according to Doctor Kelly, the angle of the wounds inflicted suggest somebody smaller than yourself was holding the knife. Somebody slight, a teenager, perhaps. Or a young lassie, even.'

'Well, I'm not the doctor, I've told you what happened, if it's my word against…'

'Is that the coat you were wearing?' said West. 'Your trusty leather jacket?'

'Aye, what of it?'

'Leather. It's remarkably tough, probably saved you from a more serious injury but, hold on, you weren't wearing it, were you?'

'I… I had it over my shoulder,' said Cameron.

'Really? You must be warm-blooded cos by all accounts it was Baltic the night you were attacked.'

Cameron, unsettled by the tense silence, leaned forward with both arms resting on his knees and rubbed his chin as though irritated by the stubble. A minute passed. Then two. Munro coughed discreetly and cast West a sideways glance, as if warning her to stay calm.

'How long had you been seeing Mary Campbell?' he said as West drew a breath.

Cameron froze.

'No comment,' he said.

'Wrong answer,' said Munro. 'Try again.'

135

'No comment.'

'Och, now I'm bored,' said Munro. 'And I'm not happy when I'm bored. Let's see if I cannae jog your memory. Did you know Mary was pregnant? No matter, I imagine you'd have dropped her like a hot potato even if you did. But see here, Don, here's the interesting thing. When the pathologist discovered she was pregnant, he felt obliged to do a few more tests, so he took a DNA sample from the foetus. Don. So, he could maybe find out who the father was. Don. And blow me down, when he checked for a match. Don. Do you know what he...'

'A few weeks,' said Cameron, angrily, 'a few weeks. It wasnae anything serious.'

'You what?' said West, seething. 'You make me sick, you know that? You're a married man, you knock off a girl half your age, get her pregnant and you think it's nothing serious? You're pathetic. So come on, who stabbed you, Don? Was it Mary Campbell? Was she pissed-off cos you'd had your fun and decided to dump her?'

Cameron stared sheepishly at the floor, flinching as West erupted in a ball of fury.

'Talk, damn you!' she yelled, her voice echoing around the room, 'Start talking or the next time we meet you're going to need a bloody good lawyer! Understand?'

Cameron buried his face in hands.

'No comment,' he said.

Munro stood and slid his chair neatly under the desk as West followed suit.

'Don,' he said quietly, 'I'm not finished with you yet. If you dinnae want to talk, that's up to you but I'm just a wee bit tired of your shenanigans, so here's the thing – unless you give me cause to look elsewhere for a suspect, I'll be away to see the fiscal first thing tomorrow and you will be charged with murder. Three counts. Got that? Enjoy your stay.'

* * *

Dougal, much to Munro's surprise, was not to be found in his usual place cowering in the gloom behind his laptops but was seated, instead, by the window with his feet up, glugging a glass of milk as he leafed through a paper packed with yesterday's news.

'I'm not sure the union allows you to take a break, does it?' said Munro.

'I think I've earned one,' said Dougal, 'I've just gone one better than Darwin.'

'You know he can't handle the cryptic clues,' said West, smiling, 'care to elaborate?'

'Okay, but before I do, will you be wanting that hotel again, only time's getting on so I'd best book it now if you do?'

'Aye, thanks,' said Munro, 'do that, would you. We'll not be travelling back tonight, that's for sure.'

'Right,' said West, zipping up her coat, 'if we're stopping here again, I need to pop out. Is there a decent department store nearby?'

'Aye, miss,' said Dougal, as he called the hotel, 'there's Hourston's down the way but if it's clothes you're after, to be honest, I doubt they'll have anything you'll like. You'd best head for the shopping centre, bottom of the high street.'

'Thanks, back in a bit.'

Munro, feeling uncharacteristically peckish, rummaged through the cupboard for something to snack on and brewed himself a mug of tea while he waited for Dougal to finish his call.

'All done, sir. They only had a double, will that be okay?' he said, snickering as the blood drained from Munro's face. 'Only kidding. Two singles, as before.'

'Dougal, I'm not a young man,' said Munro, choking on a biscuit, 'a shock like that could finish me off. Now, what's all this about Darwin?'

'The link, sir, Agnes Craig and Mary Campbell...'

'Those blessed names again.'

137

'...they were both in the same class as D.S. Cameron. They were all learning Spanish together.'

Munro eased himself into a chair, sipped his tea and stared pensively into space.

'Well, well, well,' he said as he evaluated the implications, 'Agnes too? So, there's every chance yon Lothario downstairs had his way with her as well?'

'And that's not all,' said Dougal, 'guess who the teacher is?'

'Juan Carlos? Don Quixote, perhaps?'

'Miss Jean Armour.'

'Jean...? You mean Jean Armour? Jean Armour from the bookshop?'

'One and the same.'

'Good grief,' said Munro, 'it's no wonder the man needs sleeping pills. Dougal, call the fiscal, we need to see him tomorrow morning and while you do that, have we not had Mary's things back? Her personal affects?'

'Two brown paper sacks by the door, sir.'

* * *

Munro placed the bags on the desk, peered inside the larger of the two, packed with Mary's clothes, and set it to one side. He sat down, tore open the other much smaller bag and tipped the contents onto the desk.

'Fiscal. Ten o'clock, sir,' said Dougal, as he sat opposite.

'Not much, is it?' said Munro, 'a necklace, a couple of hair grips, a ring...'

'To be honest, if she was only going round the corner to the beach to sit a while, she'd not need more than her house keys...'

'Aye, right enough.'

'Burns?' said Dougal as he picked up the book. 'Christ, I've not read Burns since I was at school.'

'Well, she must've liked her poetry, she was carrying that with her when she died, in her coat pocket. Thing is, I've seen that somewhere before.'

138

'Aye, when you found her.'

'No, no. Somewhere else. The same…'

'She had a favourite then,' said Dougal as he flicked through the pages, 'see here, this one, the title's highlighted in yellow.'

'So it is,' said Munro, taking the book. '*Highland Mary*. Not surprising, it's her namesake after all…'

Munro lowered the book and stared at Dougal.

'What is it? You look like you've seen a ghost.'

'Namesake,' said Munro, '*Highland Mary*, Burns wrote that for Mary Campbell.'

'Mary Campbell? That is a coincidence, maybe that's why she…'

'By jiminy!' said Munro, his face lighting up. 'Now I know where I've seen this book before. Dougal, have you the key to Agnes's flat?'

'Aye, it's in the…'

'Well dinnae stand there gawping, laddie! Fetch it, chop, chop. We've no time to lose.'

* * *

Munro's nose twitched disapprovingly as he caught a whiff of the musty odour hanging heavy in the stagnant air.

'It's beginning to smell like an old folks' home in here,' he said as they made their way down the hall to the bedroom.

'Smells more like my granny's house,' said Dougal. 'After she died.'

Munro took a book from the bedside table and held it up.

'*The Complete Works of Robert Burns*,' he said, 'same edition.'

'This is getting creepy,' said Dougal. 'Has he a dislike of Burns or some kind of, you know, morbid fixation?'

'Doesnae matter, either way. Look here, same yellow highlight, "Ae Fond Kiss" and you'll no doubt remember from school who that was written for.'

'No idea, but I'm going to hazard a guess it was somebody called Agnes Craig.'

'Top of the class. Okay, I need you to Google, Dougal… what's so funny?'

'Google Dougal, just sounds… sorry, what I am Googling?'

'Burns, you fool,' said Munro impatiently, as Dougal swiped his phone. 'Find out who else he had affairs with, if I'm no mistaken there'll be a…'

'I cannae believe this, I'm getting goosebumps,' said Dougal. 'The other notables in his life were Jean Armour…'

'Bookshop.'

'… Elizabeth Paton…'

'Lizzie.'

'… and May Cameron.'

'Cameron,' said Munro, 'Don's house. That's where the other copy is.'

Chapter 16

West was not a fan of flimsy, floral skirts or high heels, she wasn't prone to spending the occasional evening curled up on the sofa with a box of tissues watching a rom-com, and shopping was an activity born out of necessity which she thoroughly detested. As a consequence, her technique of tearing around the stores at breakneck speed, grabbing what she needed and heading for the checkout meant she often spent more time in conversation with the security guards at the exit than she did actually shopping. She sat sifting through a mountain of carrier bags as Munro and Dougal burst excitedly through the door.

'Thought you'd gone off and left me,' she said, dabbing moisturiser on her ruddy cheeks.

'When you said you needed a few bits,' said Munro, 'I thought you meant…'

'I'm not wearing the same clothes three days running, I feel like a tramp already and to be honest, you're beginning to look a bit rumpled yourself. Here, I got you a couple of things: shirt, socks and underwear, hope they fit.'

Munro, embarrassed, held up a pair of tartan boxer shorts.

'I don't know what to say,' he said.

'Thanks would do.'

'Aye. Sorry. Thanks, Charlie.'

'No probs,' said West, 'it's all going on expenses anyway.'

'And where did that come from?' said Munro, pointing to a large, brown paper sack beneath the shopping.

'Dunno, it was here when I got back, stuff from the Astra, I think. So, where've you two been gallivanting?'

Munro tossed the paperbacks on the desk as Dougal began rummaging through the evidence bag.

'Books?' said West. 'Why have you got three of the same?'

'Have a quick flick through,' said Munro, 'tell me what you see.'

West picked up the first and slowly fanned the pages.

'A heap of poems written in gobbledegook,' she said, 'oh, hang on, "Highland Mary", someone's scrawled over it with a felt-tip pen.'

'It was written for a Miss Mary Campbell. And if you look in another you'll find a verse penned for one Agnes Craig.'

West lowered the book and regarded Munro with a look of confusion.

'Sorry,' she said, 'the names I recognise, but the rest?'

'All these women had affairs with Burns, apart from the one to whom he was married, of course.'

'Okay, hang on,' said West, looking befuddled, 'this is the book we found on Mary, at the beach, right?'

'Correct.'

'And this one?'

'Agnes's bedroom.'

'And this one?'

'Don's place.'

'But it's blank,' said West. 'No marker pen.'

'Could be for the next victim,' said Dougal, 'or just the start of a paper trail.'

West sat back, folded her arms and sighed.

'I don't get it,' she said frowning, 'I hear what you're saying but how come there isn't one for Jean Armour then? The woman who had the hots for Max? If she's...'

'Miss,' said Dougal, grinning as he pulled a sealed, plastic bag from the sack, 'I've a funny feeling this may be it.'

Dougal opened the book and flicked through the pages.

'"Bonie Jean"' he said, holding it up, 'that was written for Jean Armour.'

'So now we have all four,' said Munro with a satisfied smile, 'I wonder what our prize will be? Some shopping vouchers, perhaps?'

'God!' said West, frustrated, 'am I missing something here? I mean, this is all great evidence but all it does is strengthen our case. I mean, what's the big deal? He's locked-up downstairs, so...'

West paused as she caught sight of Munro, wearing the slightest of smirks, gazing down at her.

'...oh, I get it. You're still not convinced, are you?'

'I'm just not willing to take a chance, Charlie,' said Munro, 'not when there's two other women who featured heavily in Burns's life who also happen to feature heavily in this investigation.'

'And they are?'

'Elizabeth Paton and May Cameron.'

'You mean Lizzie? And Don's wife? Oh, this is absurd,' said West as Dougal pulled up a chair and sat beside her, his hands clasped beneath his chin, 'and what's up with you, now?'

'I was just thinking, miss, why did he leave the books behind? After he'd killed them, I mean,' said Dougal, 'why go to all that the trouble? Why not just kill them and move on to the next one?'

'You're asking me? I don't know,' said West, 'maybe they were clues, or… or a cry for help. Maybe he wanted to get caught.'

'Or maybe they're not intended for us,' said Munro.

'Look,' said West, throwing her hands up in despair, 'ten minutes ago, this was a done deal, now… now you're making a mountain out of a molehill. Fact is, the books link Don to the victims, right? End of.'

'Maybe,' said Munro.

'Okay, I give up. What's the plan?'

'Look, with Don in custody, chances are we'll have an uneventful evening…'

'Let's hope so.'

'… but in the meantime, you'll have to indulge my scepticism if, for no other reason, than to prove me wrong. I want to keep an eye on Lizzie. If someone else is out there, then she's the one at risk.'

'Fair enough.'

'Good,' said Munro, zipping his coat. 'Dougal, have you an address for Don's sister-in-law?'

'Aye, sir. Glendale Crescent. Head down Castlehill from the station, keep going and it's on the right thereabouts, not far from the church, Saint Paul's.'

'Excellent. Charlie, you with me, we're away to have a word with Don's wife. Dougal, I want you to call Max. Now listen, kid gloves, okay? Dinnae go worrying the poor lad, just tell him he's to make sure Lizzie gets home safe, assuming she's not stopping over that is. Then I want you to get over there yourself and keep a watch on the place, discreetly mind, until she leaves.'

* * *

Munro parked beneath the hazy glow of a street lamp and peered past West at the house – a nondescript end-of-terrace, much the same as the others on the street, with a crumbling pebble-dashed exterior, a block-paved front garden without a wall, and window frames in desperate need of a coat of paint.

144

'It's a step down from the marital home,' he said quietly.

West, using tactics normally deployed by impatient delivery drivers, rang the bell several times before banging the door with the side of her fist, stopping abruptly as it flew open. Whatever a police officer's wife was meant to look like, May Cameron was not it. Munro smiled politely as he greeted the youthful thirty-something, stylishly clad in figure-hugging ski pants, Chelsea boots and a white, open-necked blouse – her neat, bottle-blonde bob framing cheekbones sharp enough to cause an injury.

'Mrs. Cameron?' he said. 'May Cameron?'

'Police?'

'D.I. Munro, Detective Sergeant West.'

'Oh well,' said May with a sigh, 'I knew that bastard would grass me up sooner or later. Hold on, I'll fetch my coat.'

'Sorry?' said West, 'I don't…'

Munro cut her short with an elbow to the ribs.

'That won't be necessary, Mrs. Cameron,' he said, 'we just need a wee chat, if it's not inconvenient.'

'Really? A wee chat? Well, in that case, you'd best come in.'

West, confused, glanced at Munro as they followed her to the lounge.

'Did he send you here?' said May as she poured herself a large gin.

'No, no,' said Munro, taking a seat, 'he's no idea we're here. Why don't you…?'

'Listen, he had it coming, okay?' said May, her kohl-rimmed eyes filled with hate. 'And I'm not sorry I did it. That philandering wee bastard deserved everything he got. And then some. Will you take a drink?'

'No, thanks all the same,' said Munro, leading her on, 'so tell me, how did this…? I mean…?'

'Okay, I'm not long home, see, when this lassie comes knocking on the door, a slip of a thing, asks straight out if Don had mentioned her to me.'

'And had he?' said West, suddenly aware of Munro's ploy.

'Are you mad? Like he'd come home and tell all about his latest conquest?'

'Point taken. So obviously, you'd never seen her before?'

'No, I had not. And I didnae warm to her either, one of those nose-in-the-air types. "We're so in love" she says, "we were made for each other" she says, "if I cannae have Don I'll never kiss another man as long as I live".'

'Be careful what you wish for, eh?'

'Right enough,' said May, taking a swig of gin. 'Anyway, then she says Don and her were moving in together and she was sorry for coming between us but hoped we could be friends. Friends! Can you believe the cheek? I should've told her she was welcome to him but I didnae.'

'And why was that?' said Munro.

'Because I'm an idiot, Inspector. All I could think was: "that's my husband you're fooling with", so I sent her packing with a few choice words ringing in her ears. I only realised later how wrong I'd been to blame her, the poor deluded thing, I mean, it's not her fault, is it? It's that cheating husband of mine. She's not the first and probably won't be the last either.'

'So,' said Munro, shooting her a look of sympathy, 'you knew about his other, shall we say, indiscretions?'

'Oh aye, and here's something else for you to chew on, he's not just been out and about chasing anything in a skirt, he's even a bairn by some tart about the place. I don't know how I put up with it for so long.'

'So it all came to a head, that night?' said West.

'Aye. I was cooking the supper, see, he comes in and I says, one of your tarts was here, she says you're moving in together so you'd best pack a bag and be on your way.'

'And what did he…?'

'You know something? That was the worst part,' said May, 'he stood there like butter wouldn't melt, denying it all, said he hadnae a clue what I was talking about. That's when I lost it.'

'You lost it?' said Munro.

'Aye. I flipped. I had the knife in my hand and I stabbed him. Sorry, but I just couldnae take it anymore. I was raging. Listen, I have bent over backwards to keep him happy. Even when I knew he was cheating, I gave him a second chance, then a third, then a fourth, but enough's enough. I'm not a doormat, Inspector.'

'Well, I cannae say I blame you, Mrs. Cameron,' said Munro. 'No-one should have to tolerate that kind of behaviour, especially in a marriage. So tell me, after you'd… he took himself off, did he? To the hospital?'

'That's right, with his tail between his legs and as soon as he got back I told him that was it. If he wasnae big enough to do the right thing, then that's me away. I packed a bag and I came here.'

'This lassie,' said Munro as he stood and moved to the window, 'the one who was going to set up home with your husband, I don't suppose she told you her name, did she?'

'Agnes something or other,' said May. 'Why? Is it important?'

Munro glanced furtively at West.

'Mrs. Cameron,' he said, 'it's possible this Agnes lassie may have been friends with a girl by the name of Campbell, similar age, blonde hair…'

'And how would I know?' said May.

'Just a thought. So, the name Campbell doesnae ring a bell? Mary Campbell?'

'Mary Campbell? I do know a Mary Campbell. And she does have blonde hair.'

'Can you tell us about her?'

'Mary Campbell is one of dying breed, Inspector. One of the nicest girls you could ever wish to meet – polite, clever, hard working. I taught her, right up until she left.'

'And where was that?'

'Belmont Academy. She's a natural. Gifted. I really wanted her to go to art school but she didnae fancy it. I was gutted.'

'Do you keep in touch?'

'Oh aye, more than ever now she's started this psychology thing, she wants to be an art therapist. Good on her.'

'So you saw her recently?'

'Took her a few bits and bobs to help her out, some brushes and paints. Why? What's Mary got to do with…?'

'Mrs. Cameron,' said West, 'I'm afraid…'

'What Detective Sergeant West is trying to say is we've taken up enough of your time already,' said Munro, 'but I do have just one more question, if that's okay?'

'Aye, go on,' said May, 'in for a penny.'

'You mentioned your husband fathered a child by somebody else. Was that recently?'

'A pregnancy takes nine months, Inspector, you figure it out.'

'No, no, I mean…'

'I know what you mean,' said May, 'I'm joking with you. The bairn cannae be more than four months old.'

'And how did they meet?'

'Burglary. At her mother's house. He was the investigating officer, only the burglary wasnae the only thing he investigated.'

'I see,' said Munro, 'listen, I know this cannae be easy for you but would you happen to know who this girl is?'

'How could I forget, Inspector. Her name's Paton. Elizabeth Paton.'

West stood up, zipped her jacket and smiled softly.

'Would you be willing to put all this in a statement?' she said. 'Everything you've just told us?'

'Too right. If it means that bastard gets what he deserves, you just tell me where and when.'

'Thanks, Mrs. Cameron, you've been most helpful,' said Munro, 'but see here, the thing is, we've not come to resolve a domestic dispute. There's no doubt your statement will strengthen the case for divorce but your husband's not actually filed a complaint against you.'

May stared at Munro, confused.

'I don't get it,' she said, 'if he's not taking any action against me, then why are you here?'

'Do you know if Don was on any medication?' said West.

'Medication?'

'That's right. Was he taking drugs of any kind? Prescription drugs, maybe?'

May laughed as she downed her drink and poured herself a second.

'Oh, so that's it. I'm not surprised, what's he got himself into now? Dealing is it?'

'No, no,' said Munro, 'we're just concerned that he may be...'

'If it's drugs you're after then I suggest you pay him a visit. He's these tiny, wee bottles he keeps trying to hide, thinks I'm stupid.'

'Any idea what it is?'

'No, and I dinnae want to know either. He's been on it for a couple of months now. Says it helps with his depression.'

'Is he depressed?' said Munro.

'Depressed, my arse. Listen, I'm no doctor but I've not heard of anyone getting over depression by sticking a needle in their groin.'

'I see.'

'And just for the record, the only medication that man ever needed was Viagra. With me, anyway.'

'Right,' said West, smirking as Munro's face began to flush, 'we'll be off then.'

'By the by, Mrs. Cameron,' said Munro as he turned for the door, 'are you stopping here tonight or have you plans to go out?'

'Go out? At this time of night? Those days are over, Inspector. No. It's pizza and bed for me, just as soon as my sister gets in.'

'She's working late?'

'No idea, probably. Just said to expect her about ten.'

'Good. We'll be in touch about your statement.'

* * *

West, head down, followed Munro at a brisk pace back to the car and waited until the doors were firmly closed before speaking.

'Well, that was a turn-up for the books,' she said, raising her eyebrows.

'Aye, wasn't it just? She's a fiery wee thing.'

'She's a gorgeous wee thing! Why the hell would Don fool around when he's got a wife like that?'

'Who knows,' said Munro, 'all I can say is, it doesnae matter how beautiful the packaging is, if you're not in love with the contents…'

'God, you're soppy,' said West, fastening her seat belt.

'Moreover, why would Don come up with such a convoluted cock and bull story about a robbery to cover for her?'

'Maybe he liked the contents after all? How come you didn't tell her about Agnes or Mary?'

'If I had, what do you think would've happened, Charlie?'

'Oh, I don't know, she'd have run off, probably. Got as far away from him as possible.'

'Exactly. No, no, the less she knows for now, the better…' said Munro as *The Good, The Bad and The Ugly* bellowed from his pocket. 'Dougal, is everything okay?'

'Aye, all good, sir. Mini-cab's just arrived for Max and Lizzie. I'm going to follow, check everything's okay.'

'Very good. Call us when you're done.'

'I don't want to worry you,' said West looking at her watch, 'but we've got precisely fourteen minutes till they stop serving at the hotel.'

'In that case, lassie,' said Munro as the tyres screeched against the tarmac, 'you'd best hold on.'

* * *

Fearing they were about to become unwittingly embroiled in an armed robbery, the young couple standing outside the hotel sharing a cigarette after what had clearly been an enjoyable evening, ran for cover as Munro slew the car to an excruciating halt beside them.

'On you go, Charlie!' he yelled. 'Grab a table quick! I'll not be long.'

'What do you want?' said West, leaping from the car.

'Anything that's not called a salad or stinks of garlic,' said Munro as he hurtled away. 'And no chilli. Or raw fish. Or anything spicy. And a large Scotch.'

West sprinted past the bar, threw her coat over a chair and called to the young girl clearing glasses from another table.

'Excuse me,' she said, almost out of breath, 'can I order, please?'

The waitress turned and regarded her with an obsequious tilt of the head.

'I'm sorry, madam,' she said, a sycophantic smile sprawled across her face, 'I'm afraid the kitchen's just…'

'No, it isn't. You serve until 9:45, right?'

'Aye, that's right.'

'Well, it's 9:42, so…'

'You must be slow; I think you'll find it's…'

'Listen,' said West, scowling as she pulled her warrant card from her back pocket, 'my watch says 9:42. The clock on the wall says 9:42. And this says the kitchen's still open, right?'

'Perhaps it is,' said the waitress, 'what would you like?'

'Two steaks, two side orders of fries, two large vodka and oranges and two large single malts.'

Munro, looking as though he'd spent the day sampling the delights of Speyside, sauntered into the restaurant, his jacket slung casually over his shoulder and joined West.

'I must've had a drink already,' he said, raising a glass, 'I appear to be seeing double. Did you manage to order?'

'Gazpacho and piri-piri sashimi. They ran out of salad.'

'Excellent. And we'll be having Imodium for dessert, I hope. Excuse me,' said Munro as he answered his phone, 'it's young Dougal.'

'Sir, just to let you know Lizzie's home safe, Max is back in his flat and I'm away to my pit.'

'Very good, Dougal. Well done.'

'Is Mrs. Cameron okay?'

'Aye, she's fine. I want you to scoot over there tomorrow and get a statement from her, she's a catalogue of capers that prove Don had affairs with both Agnes Craig and Lizzie Paton.'

'Are you joking me? Lizzie?'

'I kid you not,' said Munro as a sizzling rib-eye was set before him, 'Dougal, I have to go, my friend Angus from Aberdeen has just arrived.'

'Cheers,' said West, raising her glass, 'here's to a quiet night.'

'Your good health, Charlie. Slàinte.'

'So, I guess that's it then? For Don, I mean?'

'Certainly looks that way, unless of course the body count goes up overnight.'

'Relax,' said West, 'Don's as guilty as a fox in a hen house.'

'I hope so, Charlie. I certainly hope so.'

Chapter 17

Dougal, unable to concentrate on the report from forensics, sat staring into space musing over brown trout and the prospect of landing a couple of sixteen pounders by sundown on Sunday, when Munro's untimely arrival shook him from his reverie.

'Here you go, laddie,' he said, bearing coffee and yet more bacon toasties, 'a wee something to top-up your blood pressure and clog your arteries.'

'Thanks very much,' said Dougal, grimacing as he eyed the sandwich, 'I'll just pop it down here while I consider changing my religion.'

'Fair enough, but I wouldnae leave it unattended if I were you or yon gannet will have it away before you can say cholesterol.'

'Oi,' said West, 'bloody cheek, after all I've done for you.'

'She's right, sir. Nice shirt by the way.'

'Save the praise for my wardrobe assistant, I'm nothing but the clothes horse.'

'Did you not get breakfast at the hotel?'

'Breakfast at the hotel? Are you joking me? I've seen folk better behaved at Celtic Park during a Rangers match than that lot of a morning. No, no, this is much more civilised. So, what have you there? Another weather report?'

'Forensics,' said Dougal. 'Those bits of wool you lifted from the seat of the Astra? They match the fibres taken from Mary Campbell's fingernails and... they all came off that pea coat.'

'Excellent,' said West, slurping her coffee, 'anything else?'

'Oh aye, you're going to like this. They found some human hairs on the collar of the coat and guess what? D.S. Cameron.'

'Och, well,' said Munro, savouring his sandwich, 'they may as well screw the lid down now. I cannae see him wriggling his way out of this one. Speaking of wriggling and worms, Doctor Kelly, purveyor of pills and illicit drugs...'

'Done deal, sir. He's admitted theft and supply. Sheriff's court just as soon as.'

'Good. So, to business. Dougal, Charlie, a couple of courtesy calls, please – May Cameron and Lizzie Paton, make sure they're still breathing, would you? Then Dougal, away and get that statement off Mrs. Cameron. I'll be with Don if you need me.'

* * *

Cameron, looking as though he'd spent the night in a shop doorway with nothing for company but a bottle of cheap cider, scratched his stubble-ridden face and regarded Munro with a look of hopeless apathy.

'Well, if it isn't Mr. Pierrepoint,' he said, yawning.

Munro smirked, handed him a coffee and a sandwich, and sat down.

'How're you feeling?' he said. 'Sleep okay?'

'No. Not a wink. I dinnae have my tabs.'

'You'll survive.'

'Oh, I'm sure I will, chief,' said Cameron, tucking into his toastie. 'I'm sure I will. So, what's up? Clock's ticking, you'll have to let me go soon, unless of course…'

'Don,' said Munro, sighing heavily. 'There's something you should know. We have a meeting with the fiscal in less than three hours.'

'The fiscal? I see.'

'So, you know what that means?'

Cameron glanced at Munro, sat back and sipped his coffee.

'Aye.'

'And you've nothing to say in your defence?'

Cameron shook his head.

'Perhaps you dinnae realise just how serious this is, Don. Let me give you a wee reminder – we know you had an affair with Mary Campbell, okay? And we've DNA off the unborn child which proves it. And now she's dead.'

'So?'

'So, we also know about Agnes Craig. She was under the impression you were going to live together. And now she's dead.'

Cameron shifted nervously in his seat.

'Coincidence,' he said.

'And they were both in your Spanish class. As taught by Jean Armour. Let's not forget about Jean Armour.'

'Och, no. Let's not.'

'And guess what? She's dead too. You've a hat-trick.'

'Listen, chief,' said Cameron indignantly, 'I'm not stupid, I can see where this is going but I'm telling you, unless you have something concrete to throw at me, you dinnae have a cat's chance…'

'Trust me, Don,' snapped Munro, 'we've enough concrete to build a tower block. By the by, we know about the bairn too. Your bairn. The bairn you had with Lizzie Paton.'

Cameron hung his head and sighed.

'Okay,' he said, clearing his throat, 'even so, that's got nothing to do with…'

Munro leaned back in his chair and calmly folded his arms.

'How's the poetry, Don?' he said.

'What?'

'The poetry,' said Munro, 'you're a fan, are you not?'

'What on earth are you havering about?' said Cameron.

Munro tossed the paperback on the desk.

'Burns,' he said. 'Why the obsession?'

'Have you had a bump to the head? I cannae stand poetry.'

'It was on your bookshelf. Are you saying it's not yours?'

'No, it's not,' said Cameron. 'I mean, yes it is, but I didnae buy it. It was a gift.'

'A gift?' said Munro. 'Now why would somebody buy you *The Complete Works of Robert Burns* if you're not a fan of the bard?'

'I've no idea,' said Cameron, 'but I wouldnae know a poem if it came up and bit me on the…'

Cameron, interrupted by a frantic knock on the door, turned to find West beckoning Munro outside.

'Two minutes, Charlie, I'm nearly…'

'Now!'

'Two minutes!' said Munro. 'Don, there's no easy way of saying this but bearing in mind the present state of your… what I mean is… I'm going to recommend you for a psychiatric assessment. Okay?'

'Bring it on,' said Cameron, laughing, 'you never know, it may even help with my…'

'Oi!' said West, 'Now!'

* * *

'For goodness sake, Charlie,' said Munro as he followed her down the corridor, 'where's your manners? Are you not aware that patience is a virtue?'

'I don't give a damn who she is,' said West, bolting up the stairs, 'Lizzie Paton's been attacked, she's on her way to the hospital now.'

Chapter 18

Weather permitting, there was nothing Munro enjoyed more than whiling away the weekends with a knapsack on his back, scaling the likes of Criffel or taking a walk up the Grey Mare's Tail to Loch Skeen. A spot of leisurely hill walking, however, was one thing, scurrying up four flights of stairs was something else completely.

'Right,' he said, trying to catch a breath, 'let's have it.'

'She's unconscious but she's alive,' said West, 'but we've no idea how serious her injuries are. Her mother found her on the doorstep about forty minutes ago. Looks like she was knifed as she left the house for work.'

Dougal cowered behind his laptop and squirmed in the suffocating silence as Munro, chest heaving, walked to the window and stared down at the car park.

'Damn and blast it all to hell!' he yelled, slamming his fist on the desk. 'Everything we have, every shred of evidence is pointing irrefutably at Don, and now…'

'You should be pleased,' said West, 'I mean, you've always had your doubts about…'

'Pleased, Charlie? Another girl's been stabbed! Tell me what exactly I should be so pleased about?'

'I didn't mean it like that, I meant…'

Munro stood grinding his teeth as he glowered at West, the veins on the side of his head threatening to erupt like Mount Etna.

'Hold on,' he said, raising his hand and pointing directly at her, his voice barely more than a whisper, 'you said her mother found her this morning?'

'Apparently. Well, that's what we've been told.'

'Witnesses?'

'None.'

'So what if she wasnae attacked this morning? What if she was attacked last night?'

'Last night?' said West. 'Impossible, Max took her home in a mini-cab, there's no way she could've…'

'Dougal,' said Munro, spinning on his heels, 'you followed them, did you not see her go indoors?'

Dougal, desperate to recall the previous night's events as accurately as possible, and fearing the consequences of a wrong answer, paused as he pondered his response.

'Okay,' he said, frowning with concentration, 'I parked my scooter about six, maybe eight doors down from her house on the opposite side of the street. I saw them walk up the path together then I looked away, just for a moment, cos it looked as though they were going to have a… you know, then when I looked back, Max was walking back to the cab.'

'And the door was closed?' said Munro.

'Aye, I don't get it, sir, what are you…?'

'You couldnae see the path from where you were…?'

'No, I was too far away, and there's a wall…'

'…so there's every chance she didnae go inside. There's every chance she could've been laying slumped on the ground.'

'Oh Christ!' said Dougal, hanging his head in his hands, 'I feel so stupid, I should have…'

'It's not your fault,' said West tersely, 'you haven't done anything wrong, okay?'

'Dougal,' said Munro, 'call Max. Now. Find out where the hell he is.'

'Are you having a laugh?' said West. 'Max? You don't seriously believe he could have done it? He was at home when Jean Armour…'

'And what about Agnes?' said Munro. 'And Mary Campbell? He's freely admitted he was with them the night they were both…'

'I know, but that's just coincidence, surely?'

'I am sick to death of coincidences, Charlie!' boomed Munro as Dougal ducked for cover, 'I am drowning in coincidences! By jiminy, when I find out who killed these girls I will not be held responsible for my actions! I will personally string them up by the…'

'Sir,' said Dougal, 'no answer. It's going straight to voicemail.'

Munro took a deep breath.

'Okay,' he sighed, 'okay. Apologies for the outburst. Drama over. Dougal, get yourself to the hospital, please. Find out Lizzie's condition and dinnae leave her side, understood?'

'Sir.'

'Come on, Charlie, let's see if young Max is at home or on his way to Malaga.'

* * *

A small audience gathered outside the café on the opposite side of the street, intrigued by the sight of an old Peugeot crashing into the kerb and what appeared to be an elderly man fleeing the scene. A builder wearing a hi-vis vest and a hard hat, his arms emblazoned with more tattoos than a merchant seaman, made his way over as Munro furiously banged the door to Max's flat and shouted up at the window on the first floor.

'Is there a problem, pal?' he said, aggressively.

Munro turned to face the man who was obviously partial to more than just the occasional sausage supper and pint or six in the local pub.

'There will be,' said Munro sternly, as he flashed his warrant card, 'if I dinnae...'

'Police? Should've said. I've a size-twelve that'll get you in there if you like.'

'Much obliged,' said Munro as he stood to one side.

The builder pressed his hands against the door, testing the resistance, laughed cynically and gave it a hefty kick with his right foot. Munro smiled as it flew effortlessly off its hinges.

'As I said, much obliged.'

'Nae bother,' said the builder, 'I'll be over there if you need me.'

West stood behind Munro as they peered up the dank, unlit stairway.

'He's still not answering,' she said.

'Okay. Stay behind me,' said Munro, 'and watch your feet, there's more wildlife in yon carpet than the whole of Borneo.'

* * *

'To be honest, I'm quite relieved,' said West as they stood surveying the empty flat, 'not sure what I'd have done if he was here. Looks like he left in a hurry.'

'No, no,' said Munro, laughing as he spied a chicken carcass wallowing in a dish of congealed fat, six empty beer cans, a bowl of wilted vegetables and two plates covered in dried gravy, 'this is actually better than his normal standard of housekeeping.'

'Yugh, no wonder Dougal wanted a bath,' said West, 'hate to think what's under the bed.'

'Whatever it is, you can be sure it has a pulse.'

'Don't. Just the thought is enough to turn... what are you staring at?'

'The table, Charlie. See here, there's a spoon in the bowl of broccoli. Two knives and two forks on the plates. And a carving fork in what used to be a chicken.'

'Never realised you were an expert on cutlery,' said West. 'So what's your point?'

'What did he use to carve the chicken with?'

West, perturbed by his observation, pulled on a pair of gloves, went to the kitchen and against her better judgement poked around the empty food wrappers and cluttered draining board.

'Oi, Jimbo,' she said, holding up a knife, 'it's been cleaned and I'd say it's about the size of the blade used on Mary Campbell.'

'Now why,' said Munro, still staring at the table, 'would the knife be in the kitchen? A clean knife, when everything else is still here?'

'Perhaps he used it for something else,' said West, 'perhaps…'

The colour drained from her face as she caught sight of the figure at the top of the stairs.

'Hello, Mr. Munro,' said Max, 'this is a pleasant surprise, what are you doing here?'

'Max! Where the hell have you been?' said West.

'Shop,' said Max, holding up a pint of milk, 'have you seen what someone's done to my door? Is that why you're here?'

'No, it bloody isn't! Where's your phone? Why aren't you answering?'

'It's charging, in the bedroom. Will I fetch it?'

'That won't be necessary, Max,' said Munro, 'listen, last night, you dropped Lizzie home, is that correct?'

'Aye, of course, that's what you asked me to do, so I did. Took a taxi, only charged a fiver there and back.'

'Okay, look, I've an important question for you. When you dropped her off, did you leave her at the door or did you see her go inside?'

'She went inside, tried to drag me with her,' said Max, slightly embarrassed, 'I think she likes me.'

'So she definitely went inside and locked the door behind her?'

'Aye, ask the taxi driver if you like, we had a wee joke about it when I got back to the car. He called her a man-eater.'

'Just out of interest, Max,' said West, waving the knife, 'why is this in the kitchen and why has it been cleaned when you've not even cleared away the rest of the…'

'Dropped it on the floor. Look, I'm not proud of the fact that I'm crap at cleaning, okay, but if there's one thing I willnae do, it's touch anything once it's hit the deck. It's teeming with beasties down there.'

Munro shook his head and smiled.

'I trust you had a good evening then?'

'Most enjoyable, Mr. Munro. In fact, we're doing it again tonight, only this time I'm going to her house, to meet her mammy and the bairn.'

'Sorry Max, but I think you'll have to postpone your night out,' said Munro, remorsefully, 'I'm afraid Lizzie's been… she's in the hospital.'

'What? Are you joking me? What's happened? Is she…?'

'She's… stable. I cannae say more than that but I think she'd like you there. Will I arrange a lift?'

'No, no, you're alright,' said Max, 'I'll just grab my phone and get going. Listen, Mr. Munro, what will I do about my door? How will I…?'

'We'll take care of it. On you go.'

* * *

West stood outside the flat, glanced at the crowd across the street and turned her face to the sun, flexing the stress from her shoulders as Munro retrieved the screws from the floor of the hallway.

'Well, that's put the kybosh on that,' she said despondently, 'what the hell are we going to do now?'

'If I knew that,' said Munro as he propped the door against the wall, 'I wouldnae be standing here…'

163

'Alright pal?' said the tattooed man as he sauntered towards them. 'If you're after that young fella who just left, he's away over the bridge.'

'No, no,' said Munro, 'he's on his way to the hospital. His girlfriend's been taken ill.'

'I see, so that's why you're here. Sorry to hear that.'

'Listen, are you a builder by any chance?'

'No, I'm in a Village People tribute band, what do you think?'

Munro laughed.

'Would you be able to fix this door?' he said, pulling a £20 note from his wallet. 'I'm afraid this is all I have on me, will it be enough to cover…'

'Och, I dinnae want your money, pal. I took it down, I'll put it back. Nae bother.'

* * *

Munro, one arm on the car door, the other on the steering wheel, sat motionless, gazing pensively up the deserted street as West watched the gossiping horde of onlookers return to the warmth of the café.

'Well that's a bummer,' she said, breaking the silence. 'If it's not Max, then… unless it's a copycat but that's not really plausible, is it? And Don's locked up so…'

Munro said nothing.

'…so we've run out of suspects. What happens if another victim pops up? The press'll make mincemeat of us.'

West sighed, frustrated by the lack of response.

'Thought I might shave my head and go back to the Holy Isle, what do you reckon?' she said.

Munro turned to her and smiled.

'If the mountain won't come to Muhammed,' he said, flicking the ignition.

'They're Buddhists not Muslims.'

'You're scratching your head looking for suspects, Charlie. We should be looking for the next victim.'

'As usual,' said West, 'you've lost me.'

164

'Listen, if I'm not mistaken, there's only one possible victim left.'

'You mean May Cameron?'

'Jumping Jehoshaphat, give the girl a prize!'

'So what's the plan?'

'We keep an eye on her and let the suspect come to us. It's our only chance.'

'Okay, makes sense.'

'Glad you think so,' said Munro, 'I still need convincing myself. Ring the school, find out what time she finishes. I dinnae want to waste a whole day sitting in a car park.'

* * *

Munro sprayed the windscreen and played with the wipers, his head swaying lethargically to their squeaky, monotonous rhythm as West, her face a picture of disappointment, terminated the call.

'Called in sick,' she said, 'didn't sound herself apparently, bit hoarse and run down.'

'Well at least we know where she is.'

'Probably got that bug that's going around.'

'There's always a bug going around, Charlie. Let's hope it's not the one with a knife.'

Chapter 19

With the school run over and parents at work, Glendale Crescent, not exactly a hive of activity at the best of times, was about as lively as a Labrador on a sunny Sunday afternoon. Munro sped down the street and parked twenty yards from the house, affording himself a clear view of the front door.

'Give her a call please, Charlie,' he said, loosening his tie, 'make sure she's in.'

'Oh, right, and what am I supposed to say? "Just checking you're not dead?"'

'Make something up. Ask her if she's heard from Don's solicitor.'

West put her phone on speaker and dialled the number begrudgingly, sighing as they listened to it ring, and ring, and ring.

'Probably in the grip of some debilitating virus,' she said, hanging up. 'Out cold with a flannel stuck to her forehead. So, what do we do now?'

'We wait, Charlie. We wait.'

'Oh God,' said West, grumbling as she slid down her seat. 'Last time you said that I lost twelve pounds in weight and nearly peed myself.'

'We'll only be an hour or two…'

'Only.'

'…then we'll get some relief.'

'I'm gonna need it.'

'Have you not got any games on that smart phone of yours?'

'I imagine so.'

'Good. Then keep yourself amused while I check on Lizzie.'

* * *

Dougal, who'd not had cause to visit a hospital since he was discharged at birth, stepped from the tranquillity of Lizzie's room, overwhelmed by the intensity of the experience.

'Yes, sir?' he said timidly.

'Update please, Dougal.'

'Och, it's not pleasant, sir, not when you see it first-hand. There's tubes and wires and cables and a couple of machines that keep beeping.'

'Well, that's a good thing, laddie. It's when they stop beeping that you have to worry. So, what do we know?'

'Single stab wound to the back, sir…'

'The back? So, chances are she didnae see her assailant?'

'…probably not. She's a punctured lung and she's lost a lot of juice. They've got her heavily sedated so we'll not be able to talk to her for a wee while yet.'

'And what's the prognosis?' said Munro. 'Do they think…?'

'Aye, they reckon she'll make it,' said Dougal, 'she's still on the critical list but she's stable so, fingers crossed.'

'Good. And Max?'

'Distraught, sir, to say the least. Her mother's taken him off for a coffee with the bairn. Not the ideal way to meet your future in-laws, is it?'

'No,' said Munro. 'It certainly isn't. Okay, Dougal, listen to me: we're outside May Cameron's place. I want you to arrange some cover for yourself and come over as soon as you can.'

* * *

West, having no desire to do battle with zombies, rampage through a mythical world toting a firearm or race a sports car at two hundred miles per hour, opted instead to browse for a new pair of walking boots but soon became increasingly bored with the seemingly interminable choice available.

'How long's that been?' she said, sighing as she put the phone away. 'An hour? Hour and a half?'

'Eleven minutes,' said Munro, 'or thereabouts.'

'God, this is torture. They should rename this street Glentedious Crescent, there's absolutely nothing happening here, not even a... oh, hold up. Action. Post Office van approaching, he's slowing down and... he's speeded up again.'

'There goes your highlight of the day,' said Munro, smiling. 'Hope you enjoyed it.'

'Any second now, I'm going to climb in the back and have a kip unless... uh, just a minute, he's coming back. And he's getting out. And it looks like he's going to the house.'

'Can you see what's he carrying?' said Munro.

'It's heavy, whatever it is. Amazon, I think.'

'Probably books, then.'

'And... there's no answer. Doesn't look happy. Give him a minute, card in the letterbox and... off he goes. Back to the van.'

Munro leaned forward and gazed intently at the house.

'What's up?' said West. 'I know that look. What are you thinking?'

'When folk order something off the internet, Charlie, more often than not it's because they want it quickly. Am I right?'

'Pretty much, I'd say.'

'So generally speaking, they'd make sure someone was in to receive the parcel?'

'Yup. Oh, I see what you're getting at. Well that's probably why she threw a sickie.'

'Then why has she not answered the door?'

'Like I said, she's in bed. Too ill to get up.'

'Too ill to throw on a dressing gown and see who's knocking the door? No, no,' said Munro as he unclipped his safety belt and placed a hand on the door. 'Something's up, Charlie. Something's up and I dinnae like it. I dinnae like it all.'

* * *

West rang the doorbell and waited as Munro cupped his hands against the front window and peered into the lifeless lounge before scurrying up the drive and lifting the latch on the side gate. He called softly to West before disappearing through the gate and creeping around the small, paved garden littered with discarded camping chairs, an old bicycle and a rusting barbecue. He held a finger to his lips as she joined him, pointed out the back door hanging ajar, and ushered her back outside.

'Okay,' he said, 'get in the car and wait for Dougal, he'll not be long…'

'No, no, no,' said West, 'I'm not letting you go in there alone, it could be…'

'…do as you're told, lassie, call for an ARV too but no-one moves until I give the word, got that?'

'Got it, but you're to go no further than the kitchen till I get back. Deal?'

'Just get going before I lose my temper. Chop, chop.'

* * *

Munro eased open the back door, listened for a moment and stepped inside. The kitchen, with its clutter-free worktops, glistening hob and spotless floor was, unlike one he'd visited recently, a pleasure to behold. The faint aroma of freshly-brewed coffee lingered in the air. He placed the back of his hand against the kettle, still warm to the touch, and noted the single, yellow mug, half empty, sitting atop a coaster in the middle of the table. He walked towards the door, drawn by a deep red smudge on the paintwork, and peeked down the hallway, raising a hand as he heard Charlie enter behind him. He beckoned her forward and pointed to the waist-high crimson trail blighting the magnolia walls the length of the passageway to the foot of the stairs. West drew a breath and froze at the sound of a thud in a room above.

They padded silently down the hall and, holding their breath, stealthily made their way upstairs, taking one delicate step at a time, as though cautiously picking their way through a minefield, fearful that a worn, creaky tread lurking beneath the carpet may blow them both to pieces. Pausing on the landing, Munro placed one hand flat against the door to his right and, gripping the handle with the other, gently edged it open, sighing with relief as he discovered the front bedroom, as presentable as the bridal suite in a five-star hotel, was clear. He turned to West and nodded. Heart pounding, she stood alongside the second door with her back to the wall, wincing at the sound of a second thud. Munro slowly turned the handle, leaned back and shoved it open with a hefty shoulder barge. He stood, open-mouthed, aghast at the sight of the body lying face-down before him.

'What on earth…?' he said, recognising at once the bun on the back of the head wrapped as tightly as a haggis waiting for the pot. He knelt beside her, placed his middle finger on the side of her neck and shook his head before gently turning her over. West gawped at the wide-eyed cadaver and flinched at her blood-stained chest, the wound imperceptible beneath her blouse.

'Jennifer Clow?' she said, quietly perplexed. 'From the bookshop? What's she doing here?'

Munro turned to face West.

'More to the point, Charlie,' he said, his forehead furrowed with the deepest of frowns, 'where's May?'

'May? You don't think…'

'Let's face it, she had access to the Astra, knew where to find the ketamine and she's proved herself to be quite proficient in the ancient art of knife throwing.'

'Yes, but why?'

'Revenge? Getting her own back by polishing off every girl he had an affair with?'

West pondered the suggestion as she squatted beside Munro.

'Okay,' she said, almost whispering, 'I'll buy that, apart from one thing.'

'What's that?'

'Jennifer Clow. I can't see Don… I mean, I don't want to speak ill of the dead but look at her. She doesn't exactly fit the bill, does she?'

'Maybe not, but as we know, Charlie, looks aren't everything. Just look at his wife.'

West jumped as a muscular spasm caused Clow's foot to jerk and bang against the bath panel.

'Okay, listen carefully,' said Munro, 'get back to the car, we need an ambulance and forensics. Tell Armed Response they can stand down and get Dougal to circulate a description of May, we need to pick her up as soon as possible, then call Don, ask him if he knows where she might go if she needed to get away – parents, friends, anyone she might turn to in times of trouble. Oh, and dinnae forget to ask him if he ever had an affair with Miss Clow.'

* * *

Dougal crossed the street to chat with the driver of the 4x4 carrying the armed officers, leaving West, her heart still thumping, in the relative safety of the Peugeot to call Cameron on his mobile.

'You're late, Charlie,' he said, 'and unless you're with the fiscal, you've some explaining to do. I wouldnae want to be accused of outstaying my welcome.'

'Shut it, Don, and listen up. This is serious and I haven't got long.'

'Och, you know, you sound quite sexy when you're…'

'Oi! Listen to me. May. Your wife. Where would she go if she was in trouble?'

'What?'

'You heard,' said West. 'Has she got any friends nearby? What about her parents?'

'Has something happened to her? What's going on?'

'Just answer the bloody question! Where would she go?'

'I'm not sure,' said Cameron, 'she's not one for socialising. There's… there's a lassie at the school, a teaching assistant who works with her, she could maybe…'

'Name?'

'No idea, you'd have to ring the school.'

'Parents?'

'Miles away. Not a bad thing. Bucksburn, just outside Aberdeen.'

'Good. One last thing,' said West. 'Jennifer Clow.'

'What?'

'Jennifer Clow. Assistant Manageress at the bookshop. Did you have an affair with her?'

West pulled the phone from her ear as Cameron burst out laughing.

'What's so funny?'

'Nothing, nothing. Go on.'

'I said, did you have an affair with Jennifer Clow!'

'You have got to be kidding me,' said Cameron, still sniggering, 'why would I…?'

'Just answer the bloody question, Don!' yelled West, her patience at breaking point, 'or so help me God, I'll…'

The pause rattled West.

'Listen, hen,' said Cameron, a slight waver to his voice, 'she's not my type and I've already told you…'

'Well, you obviously know her, so that's a start. You're sounding nervous, Don. Have I hit a nerve?'

172

Cameron hesitated.

'She's my sister-in-law, okay? She's May's sister.'

West slumped back in shock and glanced towards the house as Cameron rambled on.

'I'll call you back,' she said before hanging up and bolting back inside.

* * *

Munro stood staring at the corpse – his addled mind awash with conflicting thoughts of Cameron's culpability and Max's seemingly innocent involvement in the whole scenario – and sighed despondently as he became increasingly frustrated at his inability to justify the presence of Miss Clow and, more importantly, why anyone would want to kill her.

He wandered from the bathroom, head bowed, and glanced along the landing, his eyes narrowing as they focused on the door to the second bedroom. He took a deep breath, cocked his head to one side and stood stock-still listening for signs of movement before heading warily towards it and gently wrapping his fingers around the brass handle, realising at once that it was locked from the inside.

'Who's there?' he said as he released the knob and stepped back. 'This is the police. I shall have to ask you to open the door.'

The subsequent silence played havoc with his blood pressure.

'Police!' he called again. 'This is your final warning! Open the door!'

Unwilling to rely on statins for the rest of his life and keen to avoid bypass surgery, Munro braced himself against the opposite wall, raised his right leg and aimed it directly beneath the door knob.

'Stand clear!' he yelled, cursing as he kicked it open with all the force he could muster. May Cameron was slumped against the radiator, her hands lacerated and bleeding, her white tee-shirt soaked with blood. She looked up and did her best to smile.

'At last,' she whispered, 'the cavalry, I assume?'

'May! What on Earth's happened?' said Munro, as he dived forward, fumbling for his phone.

'I grabbed the knife, silly I know, but it worked.'

'Who...? Was this Miss Clow? Did she...?'

'Aye,' said May, her eyelids fluttering, 'she tried to...'

'Dinnae pass out on me lassie, keep talking,' said Munro, as he tried to call West. 'How're you feeling? Open your eyes, look at me!'

'I'm okay, I think,' said May. 'Pissed off about the tee-shirt, it's brand new. And red never was my colour.'

Munro pulled the duvet from the bed and wrapped it around her shoulders as West came running through the door.

'Holy shit!' she said, panting. 'What the hell...?'

'Charlie! Paramedics, ambulance, now!'

West looked up at the window as the sound of sirens echoed down the street.

'Here's one I ordered earlier,' she said as she knelt beside May and held a hand in front of her face.

'How many fingers can you count, May?'

'Four.'

'Close enough. How about now?'

'Four.'

'Shit. Listen, you'll be okay, help's on the way,' she said, sighing with relief as the paramedics came thumping up the stairs.

* * *

Munro, hands clasped behind his back, watched from the window as the medics lifted May into the back of the ambulance.

'Well, that's torn it,' said West, standing in the doorway, 'two more bodies and whoever did it got clean away. Desk duty here I come.'

'Sorry, Charlie,' said Munro, distracted by the mayhem on the street below, 'what was that?'

'Nothing important. So, come on, Poirot, any ideas? Who do we look for now?'

'We're not looking for anyone, lassie. That's it.'

'What? That's it?' said West, surprised by his defeatist attitude. 'Oh come on, you can't give up just like that, what's got into you?'

'Nothing,' said Munro, wincing as he turned to face her. 'It was self-defence.'

'Self-defence?'

'Aye, May said as much. That's why she locked herself in here.'

'Ah, makes sense, I suppose. What's up with you?' said West.

'I think I've broken my foot. What do you mean, "makes sense"?'

West plonked herself on the edge of the bed and smiled smugly at Munro.

'Bet you're wondering what Clow was doing here in the first place?' she said.

'It had crossed my mind but no doubt May will be able to shed some light on that particular conundrum once she's out of danger.'

'True. Have you, er, have you ever wondered how Don met his wife? May?'

'It's not a question that's kept me up at night. What's with the cryptics, Charlie? Will you not get to the point?'

'Brace yourself,' said West, grinning, 'you won't believe this.'

Munro regarded her with a curious tilt of the head and couldn't help but smile.

'Go on,' he said, 'let's have it.'

'Jennifer Clow. She's May's sister.'

'Are you joking me?' said Munro, the smile vanishing from his face.

'And that's not all. She and Don used to… you know.'

'Are you sure? But... I mean, how on earth does a rough diamond like Don end up with Miss Prim and Proper?'

'Hear me out,' said West. 'Don was knocking off Jean Armour, right? Well, apparently Jean gave him the big heave-ho after just a couple of weeks and reading between the lines, Don, being the alpha-male he is, couldn't handle the rejection. He says he tried to make things up with her but my guess is it was probably more like harassment.'

'Let's the leave the supposition for now, Charlie, stick with the facts.'

'Okay. Clow noticed him hanging round the shop towards the end of Jean's shifts and made a beeline for him, "coffee and a shoulder" kind of thing. Caught him on the rebound.'

'Sounds more like entrapment,' said Munro. 'Even so, I still cannae see the likes of Don stepping out with Jennifer Clow.'

'They didn't,' said West, 'not according to Don. He says their relationship was purely platonic and their friendship simply gave him an excuse to go back to the bookshop and harass Jean. Clow, on the other hand, assumed they were an item.'

'Och, the poor woman. So, Don was leading her on?'

'Yup, seems so. Anyway, soon came a point when she introduced him to May. Turned out to be the biggest mistake of her life.'

'Hold on, just a wee moment, Charlie. Hold on,' said Munro, as he paced the room, scratching the back of his head. 'Where exactly are you getting all this?'

'Straight from the horse's mouth,' said West. 'When I spoke to Don, just now.'

Munro stopped pacing and sat next to West.

'Incredible,' he said as he leaned forward and cradled his head in his hands, 'incredible. Okay, go on.'

'Not much more to tell. Soon as Don clapped eyes on May, that was it, game over. Despite the fact that Clow was besotted with him, I mean, completely infatuated, she stepped aside, for the sake of her sister.'

Munro glanced at West and shook his head.

'The man's not fit to carry a badge,' he said. 'He's a snake. Aye, that's the word. A snake. I mean, just how shallow, how fickle, can one man be?'

'That's what I'm supposed to say.'

Munro stood and went to the window. Aside from Dougal sitting on his scooter and the blue and white tape flapping in the breeze, a semblance of normality had returned to the street.

'Okay, so let's think about the motive,' he said. 'There's Jennifer Clow, content to sit on the side-lines and watch her sister play happy families with the man she loves, until what? What changed? What made her see red?'

'You mean green,' said West. 'The green-eyed monster.'

'Jealousy? You think this was about revenge? A woman scorned?'

'Scorned. Unrequited love. All boils down to the same thing. I reckon, despite what she felt for Don, she was simply protecting her sister. I don't think she could tolerate seeing the way Don was treating her, with all the affairs and that, let alone the baby.'

'Aye, right enough.'

'So what I'm trying to say is, bizarrely, she was doing it for May. Let's face it, there's no way she was going to kill Don, she still loved him. But there was nothing to stop her denying anyone else the pleasure.'

'I'm not sure pleasure's the right word,' said Munro, his attention drawn to the shelves built into the alcove. 'She enjoys reading more than her sister, no arty picture books, mostly literature by the looks of it.'

'I'd go for the picture books every time,' said West, 'less taxing and no big words to skip over.'

'And looky here, *The Complete Works of Robert Burns*, same edition as the others.'

'Wonder if she got a discount for bulk. What's that one?' said West, pointing to a thick tome on the upper shelf, 'the one with the purple spine decorated with glitter and stars and stuff?'

Munro reached up and pulled it down.

'It's a photo album,' he said, opening the cover, 'and I think we'd best take it with us.'

Chapter 20

George Elliot was, on the whole, happy to go with the flow, content to let those who served under him get on with their job unhindered by diktats from above, an approach which delivered results and, generally speaking, negated the need to reprimand officers for unacceptable behaviour. It was a philosophy he applied with equal success to his home life, although without the need for disciplinary action, having learned early on in his – for the most part – "love-struck" union, that his size was no match for the wrath of a Belfast lass.

He sauntered aimlessly around the empty office, cringed at the weather forecast on Dougal's laptop, rummaged guiltily through the evidence bags as if they were stuffed with Christmas presents and bemoaned the lack of anything edible in the fridge. Lining up five mugs on the worktop, he dropped a teabag into each followed by a splash of milk, filled the kettle and checked his watch, wondering just how long he'd have to wait for somebody, anybody, to return.

West, ranting about blood sugar levels and the imminent possibility of a blackout brought about by a lack of sustenance, curbed her tongue as she and Munro bumbled through the door.

'George!' said Munro, taken aback. 'What's all this? I thought you and Mrs. Elliot were sunning yourselves on some far-flung beach?'

'Aye,' said Elliot, smiling broadly, his face a subtle shade of pink, 'we were. That is to say, we did, for a few hours at least, anyway.'

'So what brought you back so soon? I do hope your lady wife's not been taken ill?'

'No, no, nothing like that, James. Unfortunately, I'm afraid Mrs. Elliot doesnae take kindly to surprises. She decided that the sun was too hot. The sea was too cold. The food was too greasy and nobody spoke English in way that she could understand, so we came home.'

'That is a shame,' said West, 'after all the effort you went to.'

'Aye, right enough, but as they say, you cannae please all of the people, etcetera, etcetera, etcetera. Still, I said I'd make it up to her.'

'Most magnanimous of you, George,' said Munro, grinning, 'what do you have in mind?'

'Two weeks in Fair Isle or a cruise to Iceland. That way if she turns frosty, at least I'll not notice. So, come on, tea's on the brew, bring me up to speed.'

'How long have you got?' said West, looking at her watch.

'All the time in the world, Charlie. Sorry, am I holding you up? Is there somewhere you have to be?'

'Oh God, no,' said West, 'it's just that my tummy's expecting a visitor and he gets incredibly irate if he's stood up.'

'Perfect timing,' said Munro as Dougal breezed through the door, 'would you nip to the café, laddie, in all the excitement it appears we've forgotten to eat.'

'Nae bother, sir. Back in a jiff.'

Elliot set the mugs on the table and sat down.

'Five mugs,' he said, frowning, 'four of us. Where's Don? Following up a lead, I imagine?'

'Not quite,' said Munro, as he flung his coat over a chair, 'he's downstairs.'

'I see. Interrogating a suspect, no doubt?'

'Not unless he's a mirror to hand. He's waiting to be charged.'

'Oh?'

Munro sat down, locked his fingers together and stretched his arms.

'Okay, George,' he said, 'are you ready for this? See now, Don wasnae stabbed by some nutter in an off-licence as he claimed, he was stabbed by his wife who'd grown sick and tired of his indiscretions. He was also suffering from depression and got himself hooked on ketamine, which he obtained illegally, in the belief that it would help.'

'I've a sudden urge to book another flight,' said Elliot.

'Agnes Craig and Mary Campbell were both drugged with ketamine before they were killed,' said West, 'which made Don our number one suspect, not least because he'd also had affairs with the both of them.'

'Hold on,' said Elliot, frowning as he raised his hand. 'Who's Mary Campbell?'

'Ah, of course, you don't know. I'm afraid to say, sir, that Agnes Craig was just the tip of the iceberg. The body count's escalated somewhat since you've been away.'

'Australia,' said Elliot with a sigh. 'Right now, I'm thinking Australia.'

'For the record, Don also had affairs with at least two other women, both of whom worked in the bookshop on the high street: Jean Armour and Jennifer Clow.'

'Good grief.'

'And just for good measure,' said Munro, sipping his tea, 'he's a wean by somebody other than his wife. A young lass by the name of Elizabeth Paton.'

Elliot, dumbfounded, stared at West in disbelief.

'Are you sure it was ketamine he was taking and not an aphrodisiac?' he said as Dougal returned and placed a large, brown carrier bag in the middle of the desk.

'All white,' he said, 'all sausage, all brown sauce.'

'Thanks Dougal, you're a gent,' said Munro, 'tell me, George, are you fond of magic tricks?'

'Magic? No, not particularly.'

'Then grab a sandwich quick or Charlie here will make them disappear faster than a ferret down a rabbit hole.'

'Bloody cheek,' said West, helping herself, 'incidentally, sir, Don has agreed to a psychiatric assessment because of his condition. It may have a bearing on the outcome of the charge.'

'You mean diminished responsibility? He's admitted the murders?'

'No,' said Munro, 'it wasnae him.'

Elliot slumped back in his chair, a look of bewilderment on his face.

'You'll have to get me a map, James,' he said, shaking his head. 'I'm lost.'

'It was his sister-in-law, whom he also dated…'

'Good grief.'

'…before meeting his wife. It was she who introduced them. Here, take look at this.'

Munro pushed the photo album across the desk and flipped open the front cover.

'Okay,' said Elliot, 'a few snaps of Don but who's that he's with?'

'That's Miss Clow, his wife's sister,' said Munro, 'now turn the pages.'

Elliot flicked through the album as though he were perusing a catalogue on soft furnishings, a subject in which he had no interest whatsoever.

'What am I looking for, James?'

'Do you not think there's something a wee bit odd about all the other pages? Look closer. Och, George man, they're all of Don! On his own. Like they were taken without his knowledge. Turn to the last page.'

'Sorry,' said Elliot, 'all I can see is another picture of Don.'

'Aye, and he's that scar by his left eye. That's how recent it is.'

'You see,' said West, 'Miss Clow was obsessed with Don, I mean, totally, and even though she'd swallowed her pride so he could marry her sister, she'd actually never stopped loving him.'

'Until,' said Munro, 'she discovered that the man of her dreams, this paragon of virtue, was cheating on her sister. Even then, she couldnae bring herself to blame him, she convinced herself he'd been led astray by the lassies themselves, so she sought revenge.'

Elliot rubbed his eyes as if waking from a bad dream, heaved a sigh and looked pleadingly at Dougal.

'There's not a drop of Scotch lurking in yon cupboard, is there, Constable?' he said.

Dougal smiled and shook his head.

'Right,' said West, polishing off her sandwich, 'moving on. Clow knew Don was on sleeping tablets…'

'Dear God, it gets worse! Does the man not rattle when he walks?'

'…which gave her the perfect opportunity to borrow his car without him knowing. That's how she got around town and evaded detection. Then, for some reason, she grew… I don't know… impatient. Went on a bit of a rampage.'

'Sloppy is the word I'd use,' said Munro, 'aye, sloppy. She killed Jean Armour in broad daylight, in the bookstore, and attempted to murder Lizzie Paton on her own doorstep as she left for work.'

'Sounds to me,' said Elliot, his head reeling as he tried to absorb the information, 'that she's the one in need of a psychiatric assessment.'

'Aye, right enough,' said Munro, 'but it's too late for that.'

'Oh?'

'She's, er, she's no longer with us. Just this morning she attacked Don's wife but fortunately it was Clow who came off second best. May wrestled the blade from her and killed her in self-defence.'

'Are you joking me? Is she okay? May?'

'Aye, she'll pull through,' said Munro. 'She's superficial wounds to her shoulder and lower abdomen and lacerations to both hands, but nothing a spell on the side-lines won't cure. She was suffering from shock more than anything else, once they've stitched her up, she'll be on her way.'

'After-care on the NHS, eh? Second to none.'

'There'll be a hearing in due course but I'm not charging her with anything. She's done nothing wrong.'

'I need a lie down,' said Elliot, 'I'm not sure I can keep up with this.'

'We're not done yet, sir. There's something else,' said Dougal, grinning, 'and you'll not believe it. Get this – all the lassies Don got involved with shared the same name as the wife and the mistresses of Robert Burns.'

Elliot pulled a handkerchief from his pocket and mopped his brow.

'Have we any aspirin?' he said. 'My head's fair thumping just now. Robbie Burns, you say?'

'Aye, sir. Agnes Craig, Mary Campbell, Elizabeth Paton, Jean Armour and even his wife, May Cameron, née Clow.'

Elliot's eyes lit up as he glanced around the table and smiled knowingly.

'You've missed one off,' he said, disappointed to be met by a wall of blank faces. 'Och, James, surely you…? Dougal? Dear, dear, I'm surprised you're not up on your history, gentlemen, it's staring you right in the face: Jenny

Clow, of course! Born in Edinburgh, she worked for Agnes Craig. Had a bairn by Burns.'

'By jiminy,' said Munro, slapping his hand on the table as the penny dropped, 'that explains everything! Jenny Clow! It must've been around the time that Lizzie Paton gave birth that Clow began planning this. That's what kicked her off – the bairn. My God, she must have been broody.'

'Broody or not,' said Elliot, 'you've done a sterling job. I mean, for you to figure out the link with the lassies' names and Robbie Burns, that's quite a feat in itself.'

'Oh, we can't take credit for that, sir,' said West, 'it was Clow who cottoned on to that. She even tried to tell us, in her own way.'

'Well, that's by the by so far as I'm concerned. Point is, congratulations are in order. So, drinks on me. Shall we say The Smoking Goat, 6pm?'

'I'd love to, sir,' said Dougal, 'appreciate the offer but I've an early start. Fishing.'

'That's a pity, Constable, but never mind. Another time, perhaps. James, Charlie, maybe you'd prefer the Twa Dugs? More our scene, as the young folk say.'

'Not for me,' said Munro, 'there's the small matter of some paperwork needs sorting. It'll take a wee while to get all this down.'

'He's got a point, sir,' said West, 'and he's going to need a hand. Plus we have to get Don off to the sheriff's court for the drugs charge so he can be bailed and go home.'

'Oh, well,' said Elliot as he reached for his coat, 'I suppose I'll take myself off then. I need to stop by the travel agent, anyway. Before I go; James, have you any plans for the week ahead? Two maybe? In fact, let's not be shy, make that months.'

Munro sat back, folded his arms and laughed.

'Dinnae waste your breath, George,' he said, 'you forget, I'm only here as a favour to our dear departed friend, Alexander, and now I have his daughter's funeral to arrange.'

'Aye, fair enough. Fair enough. But after that?'

'After that, Criffel's not felt the underside of my boot in a quite while now and then there's the garden to attend to, not to mention…'

'Okay, okay, I get the point. What about you, Charlie? You're on the payroll now and having gone to all that effort it would be a shame to have to sort you out a P45 after just one week. And with D.S. Cameron otherwise engaged, we're a man down. I'll not deny, we could use the help.'

'I'll think about,' said West, smiling.

'Good. How long do you need? Five minutes? Ten? Will I wait outside?'

'Very funny. Can I have a few days?'

'Take as long as you like, Charlie. No pressure. Meanwhile, I'll get your desk ready.'

Chapter 21

West had designated vodka her tipple of choice ever since the demise of her engagement largely due to its undetectable status as an emotional crutch but was becoming increasingly attached to the more satisfying experience derived from sipping Munro's twelve-year-old Balvenie. She stood supervising a pan of potatoes simmering on the hob as he raised the bottle and winced, alarmed by the rate at which it appeared to be evaporating.

'There's nothing like being in your own home,' he said as he poured himself another, 'apart that is, from being in your own home with a member of the Temperance Society.'

'I know what you mean,' said West, proffering her glass, 'I can't stand hotels, you never know what the previous guests got up to and I bet they never change the sheets as often as they say they do.'

'Aye, right enough, but I'd rather not think about that just now, not before my supper.'

'Sorry. Listen, can I ask you something? Were you serious about what you said to D.C.I. Elliot? About not going back?'

'Of course,' said Munro as his phone rang in the other room, 'well, we'll have to go in on Monday to finish the paperwork, naturally, but after that, I've no reason to.'

'So, you don't fancy taking on another case? Liberating the streets of all the…'

'Charlie, are you not familiar with the definition of retirement? As I said… hold on, I see where this is going. You're having doubts, aren't you, lassie? About taking up his offer.'

'No,' said West musically, as she drove a fork through the spuds, 'I'm still…'

'You're scared, about going it alone.'

'Me? Scared? Do me a favour. Hup, there's your phone again, some cowboy's desperate to get hold of you.'

'It's after hours,' said Munro, 'whoever it is can wait. Now you listen to me, you're a grown woman, you're smart, intelligent and you're a damned good police officer, take it from someone who knows. So you accept the offer, understand? And if you get stuck, well, you can always…'

'Yeah, I know,' said West, 'give you a call if I need any help.'

'No, no. Not me, lassie, the Citizens Advice Bureau. That's what they're there for.'

West, smiling, drained the potatoes, mashed them with a dollop of butter and served them up with a couple of pies straight from the oven.

'Shame about Don,' she said as they sat at the table, 'I mean, he's a good cop, just a bit mixed-up with stuff at the moment.'

'I've no sympathy for the fellow,' said Munro, reaching for the salt, 'no sympathy at all. Call me old-fashioned, but marriage is marriage, there's no refunds and no returning faulty goods and you dinnae play around. Even if you married for the wrong reasons.'

'Well, that told me then. I wonder how Max and Lizzie are getting on?'

'Now, point in case,' said Munro, waving his knife, 'those two are made for each other, mark my words, they'll be wed soon enough and they'll not waver either. We could call in on them if you like, on Monday. See how they're getting on.'

'Yes, I think they'd like that,' said West, pointing to Munro's phone as it rang again, 'you're in demand, let's hope it's The Good.'

'Let's hope it's The Patient,' said Munro, 'I'm busy eating.'

West, pausing for a sip of Scotch, downed tools and dabbed the sides of her mouth with a tea towel.

'I don't know how you do it,' she said, 'most people fall over themselves to answer the phone as soon as it beeps, worried they might miss out.'

'Aye, well I'm not a part of the self-obsessed generation, Charlie. It's simply a question of prioritising what's important in your life and at 8pm on a Friday evening, so far as I'm concerned, my pie is more important than anything else.'

'On the other hand…,' said West as it rang again.

'Can a man not get any peace around here? Och, it's Dougal, what on earth does he want?'

'Probably just wants to say have a nice weekend.'

'Three times?' said Munro, grabbing the phone. 'Dougal, for the love of God, have you not got a home to go or some fishing tackle to sort out?'

'Sorry, sir. Is this not a good time?'

'How astute. Listen, I dinnae mean to bite your head off, laddie, but I'm trying to finish my supper.'

'Sorry, it's just that… thing is, I've had to clarify a few details before we can file the reports, you know, personal details on the victims and such like.'

'Well done, Dougal, that's very assiduous of you, I appreciate it, now take yourself off and enjoy the weekend.'

'Aye, I will, sir, thing is, I think we may have a wee problem.'

'A problem?'

'Aye. I dinnae want to sound like the harbinger of doom or spoil your supper but…'

'But what, Dougal? For goodness sake, will you not just spit it out?'

'It's Jenny Clow, sir. She doesnae have a driving licence.'

Chapter 22

Cameron, caught off-guard by the chilly night air, buttoned his coat against the sharp wind whipping off the river, made his way briskly across the bridge towards the car park on Dalblair Road and cursed as he ripped the parking tickets from the windscreen before tossing them to the ground in a fit of pique. He sat dejected and dishevelled behind the wheel, took a deep breath and wondered, momentarily, if the drugs charge would jeopardise his pension as well as his career. He glanced in the rear-view mirror and sneered at his reflection before heading home.

Wary that the neighbours would no doubt be lurking behind their Venetian blinds and chintz curtains, keen to witness the subject of a police investigation returning home, he killed the lights, pulled up outside the house and swore profusely under his breath, infuriated at the sight of the Astra sitting idle on the drive, the garage door still open.

Despite the visit from Munro and West, the house, unlike the aftermath of a burglary, did not feel violated. Just as cold, and as empty as an abandoned shell. Cameron plucked the keys hanging from the hook in the kitchen, left by the side door and returned the Astra to the garage, locking it securely before darting back inside, firing up the central heating and dashing upstairs for a much-needed shower where he noted with disdain that his entire supply of ketamine had been confiscated.

Sprawled across the sofa with a beer in hand, he stared blankly at the television as it churned out the usual fodder for those embarking on a weekend of mindless entertainment and waited patiently for the oven to heat up – a large, thin-crust pepperoni on the menu.

With no friends, acquaintances or relatives to come calling, the sound of the doorbell was an unexpected, if not unwelcome, intrusion. He peeked through the window expecting to find a neighbour on the drive, curious to know why the police had disturbed the innocent tranquillity of the neighbourhood but instead there was just a dark blue saloon parked on the street, headlights on. The doorbell rang again. Assuming it was either a mini-cab or a takeaway delivery driver relying on his sat-nav, he answered the door, hackles raised in anticipation of an argument.

'May! What the hell are you doing here?' he said, taken aback. 'Jesus, what happened to you, your hands? Are you okay?'

May, collar turned up against the icy breeze and her handbag strung across her chest, stood glowering at the spectacle before her: an unshaven specimen clad in jogging pants and a stained sweatshirt, his hair an unruly mess.

'Look at the state of that,' she said in disgust, 'I'm surprised you're still up. Have you not had your jag yet? Not filled yourself full of pills?'

'Nice to see you too.'

'I'm not stopping,' said May, coldly, 'that's my taxi. I need to collect a few things.'

'Aye, right, of course,' said Cameron, 'well dinnae stand there, get yourself inside.'

They stood in the hall, two feet between them but emotionally a million miles apart.

'Are they burned?' said Cameron, pointing at her bandaged hands, 'lifting a pot was it? Off the hob?'

'Och, save your sympathy, Don, you make me want to heave and for the record, no, they're not burned. It was my sister, wielding a knife.'

'What?'

'No need to sound so concerned, Don. Nothing's changed, I'm okay and you dinnae care about me anyway so let's not waste time talking about it. I need my passport and a few bits and bobs from the bedroom, if you havenae thrown them out.'

'No, no, of course not,' said Cameron. 'Are you... are you going away? Having yourself a wee holiday?'

'Aye. I need a break,' said May. 'From you. From here. From everyone.'

'Fair enough. Listen, are you hungry? I'm going to have some pizza just now, will you take some? It'll be ready by the time you've...'

'How do you do it?' said May. 'How the hell can you stand there acting as though nothing's happened and talk about pizza?'

'I'm only...'

'See here, Don, I'm in this mess because of you, because of your shagging around, because of the way you treat women like they were something... disposable. Dispensable. Unimportant...'

'That's not true,' said Cameron, smirking, 'and you know it.'

'No? Who've you got in there then? Another wee tart you picked up in the student union bar? Or are they too old for you now?'

'There's no-one here, I'm on my own. Listen, hen, I'm just trying to be civil here, can you not do the same?'

'No. I cannot. I need a drink.'

'There's beer in the fridge,' said Cameron, 'sorry, I'm all out of Babycham.'

'Is that whisky still in the kitchen?'

'Aye, you sort yourself out. I'll be in the other room when you're done.'

        * * *

Cameron, doing his best to remain calm, returned to the sofa and cranked up the volume on the television in an effort to drown out any noise and, more importantly, any more snide comments his estranged wife might make.

May went to the kitchen and gave it the quick once-over, checking to see if anything had moved, if anything had changed, before taking a couple of tumblers from the cupboard and pouring two generous measures of whisky.

'Here,' she said, stopping by the lounge on her way upstairs, 'for old times' sake.'

Cameron got up and took the glass.

'Cheers,' he said, knocking it back. 'Listen, May, if there's anything I can...'

'Save it, Don. I'm not interested.'

        * * *

The bedroom, without the care of a wife or a housekeeper, had transformed itself into what May imagined a recovering junkie's lodgings in a council-funded scheme would look like – the floor littered with dirty laundry, the cups on the bedside table nurturing penicillin growths and the crusty remains of a chicken chow mein festering in a foil container on the window sill.

She went to the chest of drawers, knelt down and pulled open the bottom drawer where she kept the essentials of her winter wardrobe: roll-neck sweaters, thick-knit cardigans, woolly hats and a favourite cashmere scarf. She slipped her hand beneath the clothes and rummaged around inside, retrieving first her passport, then a credit card held in joint names which they used only for emergencies and finally, an old leather purse stuffed with cash brought back from their last – and only – holiday together.

Cameron, as May had come to expect from someone who cared only about himself, was lying on the sofa, eyes

194

closed. Any concern for her welfare or the state of their marriage clearly not as important as he'd implied minutes earlier. She stood and watched as his breathing, laboured and short, caused his chest to heave, and smiled at the way his face, and then his left arm, twitched spasmodically, like a puppy in the depths of a dream.

Alone in the kitchen, May poured herself another large Scotch and downed it in one, gasping as it hit the back of her throat, before taking the empty vial of ketamine from her handbag and tossing it in the bin. She frowned as she opened the drawer, the one used for storing all manner of essential-but-rarely-used knick-knacks, before shrugging off the missing roll of black insulating tape and yanking out the drawer completely, setting it down on the worktop and releasing the nine-inch carving knife gaffer-taped to the back.

* * *

Cameron, to all intents and purposes on the verge of a coma, lay oblivious to the football commentary blaring from the television, unaware of his wife standing over him and unaware of the tip of the blade gently prodding at his throat. May moved the knife over his chest and poked it gently, deliberating over the ideal place to make the fatal incision, before jumping, startled at the sound of somebody coughing politely behind her.

'If you're not about to carve a chicken with that,' said Munro, smiling broadly, 'then I'm afraid you're in terrible trouble, Mrs. Cameron. Aye, that's the word. Trouble.'

Epilogue

'You're not listening, Inspector. How many times do I have to tell you – I didnae do it to get back at Don, I did it to get back at Jenny. Aye, that's right, Jenny. Look, those girls, those poor wee lassies, they were all innocent in this. I get that. It was Don who led them on, Don who charmed them into bed, not the other way round – but it wasnae them I was after. It was Jenny. I wanted my sister to suffer. Big time. Why? You have to ask why? Okay, look, you're probably thinking I should be thankful to her, for introducing us in the first place. Maybe. But a leopard doesnae change his spots, we'd have separated sooner or later, only she made sure it was sooner.

See here, the thing with Jenny is she wouldnae let go. She wouldnae leave us alone. If we went to the pub, she'd be there. If we went for a meal, she'd be there. If I went out for the evening with my friends, she'd turn up to sit with Don until I got home. Aye, of course she still fancied him, you know that, but there's a difference between fancying someone and being downright obsessed.

She liked her books. She thought she was better than everyone else because she was so well-read – always quoting literature, always quoting Burns. That's what gave me the idea, see. Our name. Her name. Clow. Jenny Clow.

Did you know Burns had a fling with a lassie called Jenny Clow? Aye, well, she knew that too, so have a wee guess at what her pet name for Don was. Rabbie. Makes me want to heave. "Och, Rabbie, did this" and "Rabbie did that" and "Och, Rabbie, you're so funny".

Then, when I told her about the stuck-up lassie who came calling to say Don was moving in with her, she had the cheek to tell me it was meant to be, that I should let him go, that Robbie Burns went out with an Agnes Craig. Any opportunity, she'd rub it in. So I thought, okay you wee bitch, I'll have you for this.

Did I know about the other girls? Are you stupid? Of course I did. I made it my business to find out. Everything I could. About all of them. And that's what they call serendipity, Inspector. When I discovered they all shared the same names as Burns's lovers, that's when it all came together.

Now, I'm not into reading, it bores me. I'm a creative person. I like to create things, I like to paint. I like my crafts but see, that book she bought for Don, the one on the shelf in the lounge? It's amazing how much information there is in there. You do know that was a gift for Don, don't you? From you know who? Aye, so, job done as they say. I knew you'd figure it out sooner or later. You're a clever man. And that would've been the end of it had she not gone on at me about losing him. About how there must be something wrong with me if he could attract all these other women and not find me attractive.

That's when the red mist came down. I didnae mean to kill her. That really was an accident. Death was too good for her. Too easy. But she tipped me over the edge. Not with her teasing or snide comments but with a taunting revelation. She looked so… smug.

See here, Inspector, you know how Don liked to bed the younger lassies, don't you? The students and the bar workers? Well, that's not all he liked to bed. Here's something to make your skin crawl. Did you know he often enjoyed the company of what you might call "the more mature woman"? Or rather, someone more his own age? Someone who almost mothered, if not smothered him? No, I bet you didnae see that coming.

Okay, now I've a wee question for you. Who do you suppose fitted the bill? Who do suppose was always there, willing to jump when he barked? Who do you think thought so little of herself she succumbed to his every whim?

Aye. In one, Inspector. My beloved sister. She was sleeping with him even after I'd moved out. So, there you have it. That's why I did it. And no, I'm not sorry. About Jenny, I mean. And I'll tell you this for nothing, if she's a conscience, she'll not rest in peace. She'll not rest in peace at all.

Character List

D.I. JAMES MUNRO – Shrewd, smart and cynical with an inability to embrace retirement, he has a knack for expecting the unexpected.

D.S. CHARLOTTE WEST – Racked with self-doubt after a floundering engagement, she regains her confidence with Munro as her mentor in his native Scotland.

D.S. DON CAMERON – A rough diamond with roguish appeal who plays by the book and likes to keep his skeletons locked firmly in the closet.

D.C. DOUGAL McCRAE – A clever, young introvert with more brain than brawn who'd rather be fishing than drinking in the pub.

D.C.I. GEORGE ELLIOT – Laid back and relaxed, happy behind a desk and happiest at home, he prefers to let others do the dirty work having spent a lifetime dicing with death.

ANDREW "MAX" MAXWELL STEWART – Hyper-intelligent with zero qualifications, the proverbial loner whose quest in life is to find "the answer".

AGNES CRAIG – A beautiful, passionate student with aspirations to make a difference in the world of psychology.

MARY CAMPBELL – Agnes's best friend, fellow student and a talented artist who forsakes a career as a painter for one as a therapist.

LIZZIE PATON – A strikingly attractive single mother content to bide her time as a receptionist until Mr. Right comes along.

MAY CAMERON – A sassy, sexy, art teacher whose classes attract mainly male students, tied to a copper in a loveless marriage.

JENNIFER CLOW – Officious spinster empowered by her role as an Assistant Manageress and the opportunity it provides for her to belittle her colleagues.

If you enjoyed this book, please let others know by leaving a quick review on Amazon. Also, if you spot anything untoward in the paperback, get in touch. We strive for the best quality and appreciate reader feedback.

editor@thebookfolks.com

www.thebookfolks.com

ALSO BY PETE BRASSETT

In this series:

SHE – book 1
AVARICE – book 2
DUPLICITY – book 4
TERMINUS – book 5
TALION – book 6
PERDITION – book 7

Other titles:

THE WILDER SIDE OF CHAOS
YELLOW MAN
CLAM CHOWDER AT LAFAYETTE AND SPRING
THE GIRL FROM KILKENNY
BROWN BREAD
PRAYER FOR THE DYING
KISS THE GIRLS

Made in the USA
Middletown, DE
04 May 2019